C000228332

Mac

BOOK ONE IN THE *Desert Sinners MC* SERIES

RACHEL LYN ADAMS

Copyright © 2018 by Rachel Lyn Adams

All rights reserved.

No part of this book may be reproduced in any form or by any electronic or mechanical means, including information storage and retrieval systems, without written permission from the author, except for the use of brief quotations in a book review.

This is a work of fiction. Names, characters, businesses, places, events, and incidents are either the products of the author's imagination or used in a fictitious manner. Any resemblance to actual persons, living or dead, or actual events is purely coincidental.

Mac is intended for readers 18 and older.

ACKNOWLEDGMENTS

Cover Art: T.E. Black Designs
Photography: Wander Aguiar
Cover Model: Kaz Van Der Waard
Content Editing: Underline This Editing
Copyediting: Jenn Wood at All About The Edits, Carolyn Pinard, and Andrea's Proofreading

1

KATE

The cemetery was now shrouded in darkness. Everyone had left hours ago, having paid their final respects to my grandmother. There was a reception at the house, which I assumed was still going on, but I didn't feel like talking to anyone. I was a little surprised, albeit extremely grateful, no one had come looking for me yet.

It seemed appropriate that the California sky was a dull gray and the winter sun was hiding behind equally gray clouds. I tipped my head back as the wind whipped my hair around my face. I thought of the last few months I'd watched Grandma's health decline. I'd spent most of that time taking care of her, making sure she was as comfortable as possible. It was the least I could do for the woman who took me in when her daughter had decided the burdens of this world were too difficult to carry any longer and took her own life. I'd only been six years old at the time, so my memories of my mother were few.

Unfortunately, the house my grandmother raised me in wasn't a happy one. My grandfather had been a mean, old man and when he passed away, my uncle stepped effortlessly into the role of an overbearing jerk. And while Grandma was always sweet to me, and I believe she did love me, she often deferred to what her husband and later, Uncle Stuart, wanted.

Then there was the fact that I had no idea who my father was. No one ever spoke of him, and as I got older, the only conclusion I could come to was that my father must not have wanted anything to do with me. Now, with Grandma gone, any semblance of a family had disappeared as well. I knew I needed to come to terms with that or I'd never make it. But sitting here, alone, left me numb inside.

The cold air was starting to get to me, so I decided it was time to head home. If I was lucky, everyone would be gone by the time I got there. As I stood up from the plastic folding chair provided by the funeral home, I heard the low rumble of motor-cycles driving along the road in front of the cemetery. I closed my eyes as they passed by and imagined how free it must feel riding on one of those beasts. I'd never felt free in my nearly twenty-one years.

"There you are." A familiar voice had me spinning around to look at my friend. "Why are you still here?"

"I wasn't ready to say goodbye just yet." I didn't like to lie to my only friend, but it was hard to explain to him that I would rather sit amongst the dead than be forced to deal with the living back at my house.

No one knew the truth of my home life because my uncle always waited until we were alone before yelling at me about whatever ridiculous thing pissed him off that day. Jonathan and everyone else I came into contact with assumed everything was fine. But the ugly words my uncle spewed at me on a daily basis hurt, and today, I was afraid they would break me.

"Well, it's getting late," Jonathan said. "We should probably get you home. I think most everyone has left by now."

That was a relief. I stared down at the hole in the ground, wondering what the future would hold for me. After I said a final, silent farewell to my grandmother, I grabbed my purse and started to walk toward the parking lot.

Jonathan reached out and grabbed my wrist before I got too far. "You know you can always come to me if you need anything." He tucked a piece of my hair behind my ear and then cupped my jaw with his hand.

I slowly stepped away from him. Sometimes his actions made me uncomfortable because I sensed he wasn't content with our "just friends" relationship status.

The two of us met shortly after I moved in with my grandmother. We instantly became best friends and were inseparable. In high school, we gave dating a try, but it didn't take long for me to figure out that any feelings I had for him were more brotherly than romantic. He'd said he understood, but sometimes he couldn't hide his frustration that I hadn't tried harder to make things work between us. His friendship meant the world to me, and I didn't want to lose him, so I always tried to make sure I wasn't leading him on in any way.

Since I had driven myself to the cemetery, Jonathan followed behind my beat-up sedan in his own car. My stomach knotted as we pulled up to the house I shared with just my uncle now. We lived in a little town called Apple Valley. It was a nice place, and I lived in a nice house, but what was on the inside wasn't nice at all.

Jonathan walked around to my door as I got out of my car and immediately reached for my hand as we moved toward the front door. This time, I didn't pull away because I needed to borrow some of his strength. You would think the death of Stuart's own mother would've kept him from lashing out at me. But instead, he decided an hour after she died was the perfect time to tell me exactly how he felt about me. I no longer had any doubt Stu despised my very existence. I never understood why he hated me, even when I'd tried everything in my power to be on good terms with him.

"Let's tell Stu you're home and then you can get some sleep. You have work tomorrow, right?"

I nodded my head in response. I was grateful I still had a job. My boss at the restaurant had been extremely understanding when I had to cut back my hours to care for Grandma. But, it was time to get back to my regular schedule. I needed the money so I could enroll in some college courses while continuing to pay the rent Stu had been charging me since my eighteenth birthday, almost three years ago.

I let go of Jonathan's hand and pushed the front door open.

Immediately, I could tell Stu wasn't alone. I heard the voices of his friends, Jerry and Lou. I assumed the two of them didn't have jobs, just like Stu, because they hung around the house all the time. Lou was okay, I guess, but Jerry gave me the creeps. His beady eyes were continually checking me out, and I could only stand being in a room with him for about thirty seconds before I had to make an excuse to leave.

I walked toward the kitchen to tell Stu I was home. I wanted to make it quick so I could go to my room and get things ready for tomorrow.

"Well, hello, Katie," I heard Jerry say as soon as I walked around the corner. The lecherous tone in his voice made me sick to my stomach.

I glared at the jerk, but my uncle interrupted before I could form a snarky reply.

"Where the fuck have you been?" I was accustomed to hearing the maliciousness in Stu's voice, but I'd hoped, just for today, he would be kind to me. After all, we had both lost someone special to us.

"I stayed behind at the cemetery." I tried to say it calmly. But inside, I was shaking with fury.

"Too bad you wasted your time there," he snarled back. "Now you have less time to pack your shit."

I stared at him, not sure I'd heard him right. "What?" I asked, slowly. "Pack...?"

He pointed at me, his expression ugly. "I want you gone tonight, otherwise I'll throw you and your shit out. This is *my* house now. I don't want you here, and I don't give a fuck what happens to you."

Everything around me started to go blurry, and I felt like I couldn't get my breathing under control.

"I would have done it sooner, but Mom wouldn't let me do that to her *precious* granddaughter." His hatred for me was so obvious that everyone in the room was aware of his feelings for me. He stood up; his face was red and blotchy. "I'm not supporting some stupid-ass kid my slut of a sister had no right giving birth to in the first place."

Jonathan started to lunge toward Stu. There was no way that would end well, seeing as Jerry and Lou now stood behind Stuart, just waiting for a reason to kick Jonathan's ass.

It was my turn to grab Jonathan's hand. "C'mon, there's no point in staying down here. Stu won't change his mind." I pulled Jonathan toward the stairs that led to my bedroom.

As soon as we entered my room, I plopped down on my bed and stared blankly at the ceiling. As stunned as I was, I should have anticipated something like this. I'd figured he'd tolerate me staying here as long as I paid him rent, but clearly, he despised me even more than I thought. Then again, he had enough money left over from Grandma's life insurance policy that getting rid of me wouldn't cause him any financial problems. Stu had never treated me well, but despite that, his final rejection of me stung. If there were any more tears left in me, I might have cried at how unfair it all was, but I forced myself to get through today. I could fall apart later, when I was alone.

Meanwhile, Jonathan began pacing while running his hands

over his closely cropped brown hair. I was afraid he was going to wear out the carpet. "That guy is a total asshole."

I let out a sigh and nodded my head in agreement. "He is. But there's nothing I can do about that. It's probably for the best I get out of here, anyway."

The truth was, I was scared to stay here with Stu, but I was also scared to be on my own. I didn't have much money saved, but I was taking Stu's decision as a sign it was time for me to move on to new things. I would look for a second job if I had to.

Resigned, I sat up and started looking around my room, trying to gauge how much stuff I needed to pack. I came to the sad realization it would only take my large suitcase and a few boxes to remove everything that was mine.

"You can stay at my place," Jonathan offered, kneeling in front of me. "Mom loves you and would be happy to have you there."

His mother, Louise, had always been nice to me. While I didn't want to take advantage of anyone's kindness, I wasn't exactly in a position to turn down his offer. I promised myself it was a temporary solution and my first goal would be to make enough money to find my own apartment.

"Okay," I said, trying to sound as grateful as I could, although I was hesitant and anxious at the sudden turn in my life. I stood up and looked next to my door where I noticed a few moving boxes Stu must have put in my room earlier. "At least the asshole gave me some boxes." My attempt at a joke fell flat when my voice cracked.

Jonathan and I spent the next two hours packing my belongings. Once we were done, my eyes scanned the room one last time to make sure I didn't miss anything. "I guess that's it."

I grabbed a box while Jonathan grabbed another and dragged my suitcase behind him down the stairs. I didn't bother to tell my uncle we were leaving. I had no desire to speak to him ever again.

After another trip inside to grab the remaining boxes, we loaded everything into the back of my car. It was depressing to see that all of my possessions fit inside a small trunk.

Just as I opened my car door, I remembered something my grandmother had told me about when she first got sick. "I need to run inside for one more thing. I'll be right back."

I climbed up the stairs and ran into Grandma's room. I was immediately hit with a blast of lavender. It was a scent I would always associate with her. I closed my eyes for a moment, letting the fact sink in that this was the last time I would be surrounded by the things she held dear. With one last deep inhale, I wiped the lone tear that had fallen down my face, opened her walk-in closet, and looked for the box she'd described. Back in the furthest corner sat a small, purple hatbox. I didn't bother to look inside; I would go through it later when I wasn't feeling so emotional or in such a hurry to leave.

As I walked out of her door, I ran right into a solid wall. Looking up, I met the angry glare of my uncle.

"What are you still doing here?"

He was drunk, his bloodshot eyes and the slur in his voice a dead giveaway. How did I miss the fact he was drinking earlier?

Drunk Stu was even worse than sober Stu. I needed to get out of here quickly and not say anything to set him off.

"I was grabbing one last thing. All of my stuff is already in my car. I'm leaving now." I held my breath, hoping he wouldn't take the box away from me. I wouldn't be surprised if he didn't want me to take anything from Grandma's room.

"Good. Don't need you coming back for anything after tonight." It was the only thing he said as he turned to walk down the hallway to his room.

I let out a small sigh of relief and ran down the stairs as fast as I could.

As soon as I sat down behind the steering wheel of my car, I shut the door, slammed the car into reverse, and sped away from the house I had spent a majority of my life in. I didn't look in my mirror to give it a final glance. With Grandma gone, there was nothing left tying me to that place.

2

MAC

It was well past midnight when my brothers and I finally pulled up to the clubhouse. Off to the west, the neon Las Vegas skyline lit up the dark sky like daylight. Just north of us, roaring sounds from Nellis AFB could be heard as they conducted nighttime exercises. I took a second to enjoy the windless evening as we sped through the gates of the club. I shuddered, as the chilly February night had a bite to it.

I parked my bike between our VP, Colt, and our Road Captain, Viper, and stretched as I climbed off my bike. I watched as two prospects closed the gate and secured it. The perimeter of our property was heavily gated with barbwire on top, security cameras, and lights all around. It was a fortress, and it was home.

I wanted nothing more than to head up to my room and crash, but I knew our President would want a rundown of our trip to California first. No sooner had I taken a step toward the large, brick building, when Michelle came running up to welcome me home with two other club girls hot on her heels.

"Hey, baby," she purred as she wrapped her arms around me. "Want to head up to your room?"

It grated on my nerves anytime one of the girls around here called me "baby." We weren't in a relationship and never would be. They were here strictly to keep the brothers entertained, that was it.

"Got shit to take care of first," I said as I removed her hands from my waist. "Go wait at the bar and I'll come find you later." I swatted her ass, which elicited a giggle from her, and watched as she walked back into the clubhouse.

"Let's go find Viking," Colt said as he passed me on his way inside.

I pushed my hair back off my face and followed my VP.

Viper gripped the back of my neck. "It was a good run, Mac. We'll give Prez his update, and then we can all go find a piece of ass."

I had to laugh. None of us were saints, but Viper took fucking to a whole other level.

We walked into the building and were instantly hit with loud music and dancing girls surrounded in a thick haze from various things being smoked. From the looks of it, the party had been going on for a while. In the center of the clubhouse was a large room that served as our main entertainment space. There was a bar off to the left with the entrance to the kitchen behind it. To the right were a few couches, a big screen television, and two pool tables. Down the hallway was another room where we held church. Across from that was Prez's office. Upstairs, there were several rooms for those of us who chose to live here.

Only a handful of guys lived off of the property. Viking had a house a couple of miles away, and some of the older members also had their own places nearby. They were the ones with old ladies and kids. The rest of us stayed here. It was convenient, and there was something to be said for surrounding yourself with the people who had your back, no matter what.

It was more than I had growing up.

Colt knocked on Viking's office door before we entered. It didn't matter that I'd been a member of the Desert Sinners for almost seven years and had sat in this office more times than I could count, I was always in awe of the club history that was displayed proudly in this room. Viking, along with two of his friends, Rome and Falcon, founded this club more than twenty years ago. Unfortunately, our club suffered a horrible loss five years ago, when Falcon and his old lady were killed in a crash. That was when Viking became President. Then, Rome stepped down a couple of years ago when his health started to decline, and long rides became more difficult.

Falcon's death had hit us all hard. He was like a father to me, seeing as mine was a complete piece of shit who often forgot he had a son. Falcon's youngest son, Wolf, and I were best friends all through childhood, and we even joined the Desert Sinners together. I remembered the pride Falcon showed that night. Not just for his son, but for me, as well.

As I did every time I walked into this room, I went to one of the pictures hanging on the wall. It was from the night Wolf and I were patched in. We were a couple of young dumbass kids, but the club saw something in us. *I'm the man I am today because of this family.*

Viking greeted Colt and Viper and then came over and slapped my shoulder. "So how did things go in L.A.?"

At six foot, I wasn't short, but I still had to tilt my head back to look up at the man standing next to me. He had a good six inches on me. And while his blond hair and blue eyes gave him that nice guy look, he wasn't someone you ever wanted to make an enemy of.

"Everything's good. They've asked us to increase our shipment next month."

Usually, Colt would have answered, since he was the vice president, but this was my contact, so he let me handle it.

The Desert Sinners had a hand in plenty of legit businesses to keep the cops and the Feds off our backs, but our illegal activities brought in the most money. Our largest source of income was from narcotic sales. Living just outside of Las Vegas, and having connections in Los Angeles, ensured we were never short on clients.

"Increasing the shipment shouldn't be a problem. You'll be taking the lead on that run." Viking walked around his desk and sat down in the large oak chair with Norse carvings all over. Viking took a lot of pride in his Scandinavian culture as was evident in most of his office decor. "Go ahead and get out of here. I know you all have things you'd rather be doing right now instead of talking to me after a day on your bike." He smirked at all three of us, knowing exactly what we would be doing as soon as we left.

The minute we walked out of the room, two girls latched onto Viper. "See you assholes later." He chuckled as he guided them to the stairs leading up to the bedrooms.

I walked toward the bar, feeling half exhausted and half horny as hell. I hadn't decided which need to satisfy tonight. I sat on one of the barstools and asked the prospect, who was bartending, for a beer. I took a sip from the bottle and scanned the room. That was when my eyes landed on Michelle, spinning on the pole we had installed in the corner. She was putting on a sexy as hell striptease for the group of guys surrounding her, but she kept glancing over at me. I slammed back my beer. It looked like horny was going to win out tonight.

3
KATE

It had been a week since I moved in with Jonathan and Louise, and I was feeling more unsettled than ever. I rolled over in bed and saw the big red numbers on the alarm clock letting me know I'd slept half of the morning away. The suitcase and boxes in the corner of the room were still waiting to be unpacked, but I didn't see the point since this living situation was only temporary. The purple box I'd grabbed from my grandmother's closet was sitting on top of the other boxes as I hadn't gathered the courage to open it yet, either.

I'd been working extra shifts at the restaurant, trying to make up for the hours I'd missed during the prior months. I would come back here every night, barely able to keep my eyes open and too drained to deal with whatever emotions might come from seeing what Grandma had put aside for me.

"Hey, Katie." I looked up and saw Jonathan standing in the

doorway of the guestroom. He was always so chipper in the morning, and it drove me crazy. I'd never been a morning person.

"Hey." The brightness in his eyes dimmed just a bit at my lackluster response to his greeting.

"Do you have any plans today? I have the day off and thought we could finally hang out." He walked over and sat down on the edge of the mattress.

"I don't know, Jonathan. I've been exhausted." I'd been blowing him off, and I felt terrible, but I didn't have it in me to be sociable right now.

"We haven't hung out in weeks," he complained, his expression downcast and his shoulders slumping a little. "I miss my best friend."

And just like that, I felt guilty for ignoring him. He'd been nothing but kind while I wallowed in self-pity.

I could admit that our friendship became a bit one-sided when Grandma had gotten sick. I put all my time and effort into taking care of her. Any extra time was spent working so I could continue to pay my bills. Seeing the disappointment on Jonathan's face now made me realize things needed to change. I couldn't take for granted the one remaining relationship I had left.

"You're right. I'm sorry I've disappeared on you. How about we go out tonight around six for pizza? My treat," I offered with a big smile.

"Sounds like a plan." He leaned over and kissed my forehead. "What are you going to do until then?"

"I have a couple of errands to run, and I should probably unpack my clothes at least."

"Okay," he said, clearly elated at my offer to hang out tonight. "If you need anything, you know where to find me. I promised my mom I would take care of the yard work today."

Ever since Jonathan's father left, he'd done whatever he could to help his mom out. It was why he continued to live at home with her, and I admired his dedication and loyalty. But sometimes, it was hard being around them. I longed for that type of family connection, a parent who gave a damn about me and loved me unconditionally.

I took my time getting ready and went about running the few errands I had. After a quick trip to the grocery store to pick up a few personal items, and a stop at the cell phone store so I could pay my bill, I found myself back at Jonathan's house.

"Hello?" Louise called out when I opened the front door.

"Hi, it's just me," I returned and made a detour into the kitchen where she was busy washing dishes.

I put my bags down on the dining table and walked over to her. I picked up a towel and started drying the plates in the rack.

"Jonathan told me you guys had plans tonight, so I'm guessing you won't be here for dinner?" she asked excitedly, reading far too much into the situation.

Louise had probably been the most upset when Jonathan and I decided only to be friends. I hated disappointing her, but I couldn't be with someone just because those around us thought we were meant to be together.

"Yeah, we're going to go out and grab some pizza tonight.

I've been a bad friend lately. Figured pizza might get me back in his good graces." I emphasized the friend part, in an effort not to get her hopes up. I didn't want her to think anything else was going on.

"It usually does the trick." We both laughed at the fact that Jonathan was so easygoing that almost anything could be forgiven just by feeding him.

I put away the last dish and grabbed my bags so I could head up to my room.

"Thanks for the help, sweetie."

"Any time," I responded as I walked out of the kitchen.

I put away the toiletries I'd bought and then sat on my bed, staring at the boxes I'd stacked in the corner. I had another hour before Jonathan and I were leaving, so I figured now was as good a time as any to go through the box Grandma had left for me.

I walked over to the stack of boxes and grabbed the one on top. It wasn't very heavy, but I could hear a few items rattling around inside. I sat back down on my bed and stared at it for a few minutes. Suddenly, my palms felt sweaty, and I could feel my heart nearly beating out of my chest. I wasn't ready for this. I felt like as soon as I opened the box, it would be the final thing letting me know Grandma really was gone.

That sounded stupid because I'd been in bed with her when she took her final breath. I knew she wasn't coming back, but it hadn't hit me yet. I'd kept myself busy with funeral arrangements, and now work, so I wouldn't sit around and think about never seeing her again.

I didn't want to acknowledge that I was really alone now. It was a depressing thought, and I didn't want to get caught in that downward spiral.

I took a deep breath as I lifted off the top of the box. I could feel the stinging in my eyes the minute I looked at the photo sitting on top of everything else inside. It was a picture of my grandmother, Mom, and me. I couldn't have been more than four years old. It looked like we were at a park, and the three of us were all smiling. I had no idea who had taken that picture. I couldn't imagine it was my grandfather or uncle. They never spent time with us like that.

Seeing photos of my mom was always odd. I looked nothing like her. Where her hair was brown, mine was blonde. Her green eyes were dark and mysterious, while my eyes were bright blue. I knew I must have inherited those features from my father, but it felt strange to think I looked like someone I'd never met.

"Oh, crap," I muttered to myself. Seeing that picture made me realize I'd left an entire box of photos hidden under my bed. I'd been in such a hurry to leave, I had completely forgotten about them. I used to look at pictures of my mother all the time when I was younger, until my grandfather caught me once and yelled at me for crying over a dead woman who hadn't loved me enough to stick around. Those were his words, not mine, but they had a profound effect on me growing up.

I had to get those pictures back, but Stu had made it clear I wasn't welcome there anymore. I would need to think of a way to get those back someday.

I put the photo aside and started looking through some of the other items. My grandmother had saved the baby book my mom had begun to fill out. I flipped through the pages, smiling at the random things she decided were important enough to commemorate in there.

Toward the bottom of the box, there was a large envelope labeled "For Kate," in my grandmother's cursive handwriting. Confused, I opened the flap and shook out what was inside.

It was a letter folded in half, three pages long. The paper was soft and faded, like it'd been handled many times before. *By Grandma?* That gave me pause, wondering if that had been the case, why she'd never said anything to me. I shook my head and unfolded the letter, which had handwriting I didn't recognize but quickly realized had to be my mother's.

The ink on the letter was slightly gray, and there were random smudges all over the first page.

Dear Katie Bug,

I can still remember feeling your little feet kicking, so antsy to be free and so full of life.

You're a miracle. My little miracle, the one thing that truly made me happy to be alive. The only thing that ever mattered to me in this unhappy world of mine.

There were days when I was sad, and everything was overwhelming, but you somehow made all the bad thoughts and feelings disappear with just a smile. I wished for so much when you were born, for you to have all the things I never had...

Hot tears were streaming down my cheeks, but I didn't

attempt to wipe them away. When I'd opened the box, I hadn't expected to find anything left of my mother, and my chest hurt with an old loss I'd never fully reconciled. Grandma never spoke about her after she'd killed herself, not even on her deathbed. I supposed the grief had always been too painful, even after all these years.

I took a deep, calming breath and continued onto the next page of the letter:

I am so sorry for leaving you. Being your mom was the only thing that ever brought me any joy. Please know that I love you with all of my heart, but I just couldn't go on.

You have done nothing wrong, my perfect little girl. And I hope, someday, you'll understand that this was my choice and my choice alone. There was nothing you or your grandma could have done—it was just my time.

My only regret is that I won't see the beautiful woman you'll become but I will watch from above in Heaven. I will always be with you in spirit, never doubt that...

Lastly, I wanted to apologize for never having told you about your father. I know you'll be curious about him as you grow up. I met him when I was young and stupid. Your grandparents thought it was best to keep your father's identity a secret from you considering the kind of man he was and the people he associated with. It seemed sensible at the time, and I was scared, but now, I don't know if that was the right thing to do.

Enclosed is your birth certificate. His name is listed as

your father if you decide to search for him once you're an adult. He didn't abandon you—I never told him you existed. Last I knew, he was living just outside of Las Vegas. If you can find a motorcycle club called the Desert Sinners, you should be able to find him.

I wish you all the happiness in the world. You deserve nothing less than being happy and loved.

Love, Mom

My vision blurred, my tears creating dots all over the letter, which I now wondered if the smudges were created by the tears of my mother when she wrote this final letter. This letter was her suicide note—to me.

I held the letter against my chest, sobbing. My entire world was once again flipped upside down. Sniffing, I wiped at my eyes and re-read the letter at least a half dozen more times until I'd calmed down. I never thought anyone would give me any information about my father. So many questions swarmed my clogged and tired brain. Did I want to know anything about him? Or had so much time passed that it didn't matter anymore? What if I did find him? Would he accept me or toss me away, as I'd always assumed he had? Fear and hope clouded every one of my thoughts. But to know I had *family* out there...the possibilities were overwhelming.

The third page was, indeed, my birth certificate. My hands were shaking, and my heartbeat sounded loud in my ears as my eyes scanned the whole document. There it was...all the information regarding my birth. I saw my name *Kathryn Marie Nixon* and my birthday of March 26th. A couple of lines further down, I saw what I had never known before, my father's name. *Samuel Andersen.*

I waited to see if I felt any different, finally knowing his name after almost twenty-one years. But I didn't. I was still me, except now I had this information that I had no clue what to do with.

There wasn't much else in the box. Mostly birthday cards and a couple of trinkets from when I was a kid. At the very bottom was a small, heart-shaped locket attached to a chain. When I opened it, I saw a picture of my mom on one side and a picture of me on the other. I unclasped the necklace and put it on. It was simple yet beautiful.

I put everything except my birth certificate back into the box. I placed the document on my bedside table. I would decide later what to do with that information.

Mindlessly, I unpacked my suitcase and put away my clothes in the small dresser. A look at the clock told me I only had twenty minutes before Jonathan and I were supposed to go out. I took a quick shower, threw my hair up in a messy bun, put on minimal makeup—mostly to hide the redness from crying—then dressed in jeans and a sweater.

Right on time, I heard a knock on my door.

"Come in," I said as I pulled on my brown boots.

Jonathan walked in. "You ready to go?" he asked.

I grabbed my purse. "Yep."

The drive to the pizza parlor was quieter than usual, and I felt responsible for things becoming somewhat strained between the two of us. I vowed to make an effort to remedy that.

We walked into the restaurant, placed our order at the counter, and found a booth in the corner. We made small talk for a bit, which only made the evening feel that much more awkward. It didn't help that I was distracted by my mom's letter too. Jonathan must have noticed as well.

"Everything okay? You seem distant tonight."

"Um..."

I didn't know if I was ready to share what I had found out about my father with anyone yet, but this was Jonathan. He had been there for me during every hard time in my life. Maybe he could help me figure out what to do.

"You know that box I grabbed out of my grandmother's closet?"

He nodded his head, so I continued.

"Well, I opened it today. There was information about my father in there."

Just then, the server brought the pizza to our table. We thanked him and then I turned back to Jonathan. He was staring at me with wide eyes.

"Well, what did it say?" he asked, our food momentarily forgotten.

I gave a brief explanation. "I have a name and a general idea of where he might be living," I added, keeping the fact that he could be part of a motorcycle club to myself for now.

Jonathan could be pretty closed-minded about people, one of

the things that drove me crazy, so I didn't think he would be thrilled with that detail. Especially if I decide to meet my father.

"What are you going to do?" he finally asked. I scrutinized him carefully to see if I could figure out what he thought I should do, but his face gave nothing away.

"I'm not sure." I shrugged, pretending like it wasn't a big deal.

"He may not have abandoned you, but you've managed to get this far without him," he said, somewhat dismissively, as he began diving into the pizza. "Maybe it would be best to leave well enough alone."

I didn't meet Jonathan's eyes when they swept over me. "Maybe," I murmured, wishing he'd said the exact opposite and knowing it wasn't a matter of *if* I'd meet my father, but *when*.

4

KATE

A few days had passed since I found out about my father, and I wasn't any closer to deciding what I wanted to do. Jonathan didn't share any words of wisdom about the situation when we'd talked about it, but I did feel like we had made some progress in getting our friendship back on track. We had ended that night watching a movie in my room, where we both fell asleep about fifteen minutes into it.

Even with the uncertainty surrounding my father, the last week had been filled with ease and a sense of contentment. Maybe I didn't need to mess with that by seeking out a man I knew nothing about. The possibility of being rejected was more than my heart could handle right now.

It was a little after ten, and I'd just finished my shift at the restaurant. I was bone tired, but Jonathan and I had plans for another movie night after I got home from work. I just hoped we could make it past the first scene this time.

When I walked into my room, I was surprised to see Jonathan already reclining on my bed, a bowl of popcorn next to him.

"Hi, there," I greeted.

"Hey! Glad you're home. Thought I would go ahead and get everything ready," he said, stating the obvious.

"Thanks." I grabbed my pajamas out of the dresser drawer and walked across the hallway to the bathroom so I could wash my face and change.

When I came back into the room, I climbed in the other side of the bed and snuggled under the covers, ready to watch whatever movie he'd selected. When it started playing, I was shocked he'd picked a romantic comedy. Usually, I was subjected to some action flick when it was his turn to pick what we watched.

"This is different." I elbowed him in the side, laughing at his selection.

"Yeah." He shrugged his shoulders. "I thought I would change it up a bit." He was acting a bit strange, almost like he was nervous. I decided to not worry about it and settled in for a relaxing night with my friend.

An hour later, we'd finished the popcorn, so Jonathan moved the bowl over to the bedside table. I snuggled further down into my blankets as my eyes started to feel heavy. I was comfortable and sleepy, but determined to stay awake and finish the movie.

Without warning, Jonathan turned toward me and slammed his lips against mine.

I pushed at his shoulders and turned my head away. "What the hell are you doing?" I growled at him.

"Come on, Katie." He leaned over the top of me, but I pushed him away once again. "I don't get it. I've given you space, but lately, you've been spending all of your free time with me. We fell asleep together almost every night this week. Why are you fighting this?"

I sat up, trying to put more space between us. "We do those things because I thought you were my best friend. We tried this before; it didn't work."

"Seriously? I do everything for you!" he said, clearly frustrated. "You've put me in the boyfriend role, but I don't get to reap any of the benefits. I've turned down other girls because I figured you just needed some time." He jumped out of bed and ran his hand over his head. "You've been leading me on this whole time."

I couldn't contain the shocked gasp that left my mouth. "What are you talking about? I've never led you on."

"Oh, really?" he shot back sarcastically. "You're always holding my hand, cuddling with me at night. You're a giant cocktease." He was starting to shout at me, and I was afraid he was going to wake Louise.

"I think you need to leave my room before either of us say anything else we might regret," I said as composed as I could manage. For the first time since I'd known Jonathan, he was scaring me.

"Whatever," he snarled back, and spun around. He, of course, made sure to slam my door as he walked away.

Trembling, I flopped back down on my bed. I wasn't sure where his outburst had come from. Jonathan had never acted that way toward me before. Calling me a cocktease was ridiculous. I wasn't acting any differently than I had during the past several years of our friendship. Even if he'd mistaken my acts of friendship as more, he had no right to try anything on me. He was the one person in my life who felt stable, and now that was all gone.

What hurt me the most, though, was when he said he did everything for me. Sure, in the last couple of months, I was the more needy friend in our relationship, but friendships often went through phases where one person needed more support than the other. There had been plenty of times when I was the one helping him. Like when his father decided to leave him and his mother, or the month that I pushed him around in a wheelchair after he had broken both of his legs in a skiing accident. Since when had he expected something in return, when all he should have expected was a friend when he needed one—and vice-versa? It seemed, no matter what, I couldn't catch a break, and it was starting to wear me down at every level.

As I pulled the covers over me, I couldn't help but think it was going to be damn hard for our friendship to recover from our argument. Not only was I sad about that, but I also realized I needed to find a new place to live, sooner rather than later. We clearly couldn't continue living under the same roof. Apparently, I would be spending my day off tomorrow searching ads for rooms to rent. I closed my eyes, recalling my mother's words of her watching over me. I hoped it was true, and that I actually had someone in my corner, no matter what. Lord knew I needed it.

That night, I had slept so poorly, that when I woke the next morning, I had a pounding headache. The words from my fight with Jonathan were running through my mind, and I was trying to figure out why everything was going horribly wrong. I'd hoped Jonathan would come by this morning to apologize, but judging by the time, he'd already left for work. Same for Louise. At least there wouldn't be any awkward questions to make things worse.

Maybe it was better he wasn't here. I could come up with a plan and then talk to him later. I glanced over at my bedside table, the folded up piece of paper catching my eye. Everything suddenly clicked into place.

After I got dressed and had breakfast, I logged on to Louise's computer and did a general search for "Desert Sinners." I was relieved to find they really did exist, but, to my unease, I mostly found newspaper articles about their dealings with the law...and they seemed to always be on the wrong side of it. There was no mention of a "Samuel Andersen," which gave me pause. Even if he wasn't a part of their organization, though, I figured someone would have heard of him and could point me in the right direction.

As the day wore on, I battled with the pros and cons of my decision; but, deep down, I knew there was no other path for me. Grandma's death, coupled with the recent development with Jonathan, was exactly the push I needed to go out on my own and find what would make me happy.

After lunch, I checked my bank balance on my phone app. I had enough saved up that I could afford a cheap motel for a couple of weeks. Given the number of restaurants in Las Vegas, I figured I could find a job relatively easy if I wanted to extend my time there.

I re-packed all my stuff, and then wrote a note to Louise and Jonathan explaining my plans. I knew it was awful of me not to wait the few hours until they got home to tell them in person, but I knew if I waited, one of them would convince me to stay. I explained that in the letter, and hoped they'd be forgiving and accepting of my decision.

Once I put my stuff in the car, I got behind the wheel, and took a deep, steadying breath to calm my nerves. I looked out the window. The sky was blue and the sun, warm and bright.

"Here I go, Mama," I whispered before starting the car and pointing it eastward. "Please watch over me…"

Like the last time, I didn't look back. I had no choice but to keep moving forward.

5

MAC

It was a usual Friday night at the clubhouse. Tons of people, loud music, and enough alcohol to ensure none of us would end the night sober. Earlier in the day, we had a barbeque for the families. After we ate, the old ladies and kids headed back home. Some of the brothers did as well, including Viking. He didn't give a shit what kind of debauchery was going on, but he didn't participate in it.

Viking and his wife, Meredith, had been together for almost twenty years. They were the real deal, and he wouldn't think of fucking that up by messing around with a piece of club ass.

As the night progressed, some of the local chicks had come out to party, so there was plenty of pussy to go around, but I was bored. Michelle kept approaching me, but I'd fucked her twice in the last week. Anything more than that and she would start thinking we were in some sort of relationship.

Fuck that.

"See anything worthwhile?" Wolf slapped me on the back and sat down on the barstool next to me.

"Not yet." One of our prospects, Zeke, was bartending tonight. I signaled for him to come over and ordered two more shots. "A few more of these and I'm sure something will catch my eye."

"You ready to ride out in a few days?" my friend asked as we continued to scan the crowd.

I nodded, picking up the pack of smokes lying on the bar, taking out a cigarette, and lighting it with my Zippo. "Absolutely."

Our next trip was going to be our first weapons run. One of our brothers, Spike, had been working on the deal for a while. A rival club, the Phantoms, was heavily involved in the gun trade, and they were trying to make a move on our territory. If we could secure the gun market, then we could protect our territory and ourselves.

Wolf and I continued to shoot the shit for a while before we were interrupted by TJ, one of our other prospects.

"Anyone seen Colt around?"

"He's probably in his room fucking his first girl of the night," Wolf informed him. "What's up?"

"There's some chick out front looking for Viking. Figured since he already left, maybe Colt could deal with her."

"What do you mean by *some chick*?" It didn't make sense to me that a woman was here looking for Viking. He stayed clear of any kind of drama, especially the kind involving crazy bitches.

"I don't know, man. She's pretty young, and she wouldn't tell me what she needed to speak to him about. That's why I didn't let her in."

"Good man," I said as I stood up and walked past him. "I'll go check it out."

Usually, Colt would handle things when Viking was unavailable, but as the secretary of this club, I could deal with some girl.

I opened the door and was hit with a blast of cold air. We may live in the desert, but it was cold as fuck at night in the winter. I looked around but didn't see anyone.

I was just about to go back inside when movement off to the right caught my eye. Whoever was there slowly made their way closer to me. Once she was standing under the glow of the porch light, I could make out most of her features.

She was tall for a female, at least five-foot-nine. She had long, blonde hair that almost reached her waist. Her bright-blue eyes were huge, and she looked like she was ready to bolt at any minute. That wasn't surprising. The clubhouse didn't exactly have a welcoming vibe to it.

Even though she looked scared, I couldn't ignore how hot she was. Her sweater and jeans couldn't hide the fact she had big tits with a tiny waist and the longest pair of legs I'd ever seen. I had no idea what someone like her would want with Viking, but I was willing to let her wrap those sexy legs around me.

She took two more steps toward me, and that was when I noticed how young she looked. I wasn't sure if she was even legal. That was enough to quickly kill any thought I had of making her mine for the night.

"You're the chick looking for Viking?" I asked, not caring if my gruff voice scared her more than she already was. We didn't need anyone causing trouble for the club.

"Viking?" she asked, her voice shaky, giving me a confused look.

I squinted at her, my guard up. "Yeah, the president of this club," I said, slowly. "That's who you were asking for, right?"

Her eyes darted around like a caged animal. "I don't know who Viking is. I'm looking for a Samuel Andersen."

What the hell? No one ever referred to Viking by his legal name. I had no clue what this girl was up to, but I wasn't going to give her any information until I found out.

"Sorry to break it to you, sweetheart, but there's no one here by that name."

"Please, I need to find him. I have something important to tell him." She stood there, looking at me with pleading eyes.

"I'm going to need more from you before I help you out," I responded, standing back with my arms crossed over my chest while I slowly eyed her up and down.

A loud gasp escaped her as she moved back quickly, and I knew what she must have thought I was insinuating.

"Don't flatter yourself, sweetheart. You're not my type," I lied.

Her shoulders slumped, and I couldn't tell if it was in relief or disappointment.

"Are you going to be able to help me or not?" she asked in a huff.

I had to give her credit; she wasn't backing down, even

though I was acting like a dick. "That's up to you. Are you going to tell me why you're looking for Viking?"

"Um..." she started, her bravado gone.

I turned away, opening the door to walk back into the club-house, but she reached out and grabbed hold of my arm before I could step through. I looked down at her small hand on my bicep and then back at her. She turned white as a ghost when she realized she had touched me. She pulled her hand back quickly like I'd burned her.

"I...I'm sorry. It's just"—I could tell she was struggling with whether she should level with me or keep her secrets—"he's my father."

"Bullshit!" I yelled while she stumbled back, the door slamming closed behind us. There was no way Viking ever cheated on Meredith, and he definitely didn't have a kid out there that no one knew about.

"It's not bullshit!" she shouted back, almost hysterical. "I just found out a few days ago, when I was going through some of my grandmother's stuff. There was a birth certificate that had a Samuel Andersen listed as my father. A letter from my mom said he was a Desert Sinner."

"How old are you?" I asked, keeping my bark to a minimum, though she still jumped a little.

"I'll be twenty-one next month."

Well, shit. She would have been born before Viking got with Meredith. Maybe the girl wasn't full of shit. She also wasn't as young as I thought, not that it changed anything if she was Viking's daughter.

"So...can I talk to him, *please*?"

I went still, hesitating a little. It was the desperate way she said "please" that caught me off guard somewhat. I hadn't heard that kind of despair since I was a kid myself, begging for my own parents not to toss me aside like Sunday's garbage.

"I can't promise anything, but come on inside, and I'll see what I can do," I offered, not sure why I was being nice, even though I didn't like the situation at all.

"Okay," she agreed, but didn't make any move to enter the clubhouse when I opened the door again.

"I'm not going to stand out here all night," I said, my voice low, getting irritated and not bothering to hide it.

Before she brushed past me, I gripped her upper arm firmly, stopping her. She winced and looked at me. "What now?" she asked, a mix of weariness and fear in her tone.

"What's your name?"

"It's Kate," she said after a long pause.

"Kate..." I repeated. Pretty name, pretty girl. Why I'd asked, I didn't really know. I loosened my grip and gestured with my head for her to continue inside. She didn't hesitate this time. I followed her in and rather too closely when she suddenly stopped. I had to place my hands at her narrow waist to stop my momentum from crashing into her, and I couldn't lie, I didn't mind the contact. It was obvious she was more shocked by the loud party going on in front of her than me touching her.

"Maybe I should come back another time," she said.

I squeezed her waist and pushed her forward. "Not so quick, you're already here. Might as well get this settled now."

I directed her over to the bar where Wolf was still hanging out, albeit now with a chick grinding her ass against his dick. Kate's eyes were wide as she took in the activities happening all around us. There was a couple having sex on the pool table, another girl dancing on the pole, and a couple of people getting high over in the corner.

Wolf looked at the girl standing next to me, then gave me a *what the fuck* look.

"Go sit there," I ordered, pointing to a lonely chair by the bar. She gave me a look but did as I instructed.

I motioned for Wolf to come talk to me. He got up, much to the disappointment of the chick still vying for his attention.

I explained quickly what I'd learned outside. He seemed as shocked as I was.

"What are you going to do?" he asked me, but kept his eyes on our visitor.

"I'm going to go pull Colt out of whatever hole he's found himself in, and I was hoping you'd call Viking."

"On it," he said as he walked toward the front door.

I eyed Kate, who was keeping her shit together for now, but she looked completely out of place. I motioned Zeke over. "Watch her and don't let anyone mess with her. I'll be right back."

I ran upstairs to Colt's room where I banged on the door.

"Go away!" our VP yelled.

"Dude, we have a situation."

I could hear some angry mumbling before the door was

thrown open. "This better be good," he grumbled while zipping up his pants.

I peeked around Colt and saw Michelle and one of the other club girls sitting naked on his bed. The one whose name I didn't know was glaring at me, pissed I had interrupted her good time. When I glanced at Michelle, she had a little smirk on her face. I didn't know what kind of game she was playing, but if she thought I was going to be jealous of her fucking Colt, she had another thing coming. I didn't give a shit who she was with.

I turned my attention back to Colt. "Wolf's calling Viking, but I thought you should come on down for this."

That got his attention, and his demeanor quickly shifted from pissed to alert. I filled him in on what was going on as we made our way down the stairs.

I looked over at the bar and was relieved to see Kate still sitting there. Wolf was talking to her now, and she looked just as freaked out as she'd been while talking to me outside.

"Viking's on his way. I didn't tell him anything, just that we needed to talk to him ASAP. He wasn't thrilled," Wolf explained when we reached them.

I saw our visitor blanch at his words. I'm sure she was questioning her decision to step foot on this property.

"All right, sweetheart, what's this all about?" Colt asked.

She glared at all of us then at Colt. "My name is Kate, not sweetheart." She said the last part under her breath.

"Well, Kate, let's head out to the backyard," Colt said, lips twitching at her spunky attitude. "It's quieter outside, and I know Viking won't want an audience for this conversation."

She went pale but asked, "Why do you keep calling him Viking?"

It was clear this chick knew nothing about our lifestyle. Based on her reaction, she'd lived a very sheltered life. I was all too familiar with girls like her and knew she wasn't cut out to hang around guys like us.

"It's a road name," I answered. "Any other questions, I suggest you wait and ask him."

I grabbed a couple of beers off the bar and led Kate outside. Wolf stayed inside to wait for Viking, but Colt silently followed behind us. He was a man of few words, but he took everything in. He probably already had a good read on this girl.

"I didn't mean to make him angry. Maybe I should come back another time," Kate said, sounding defeated as we stepped into the backyard.

"Now's as good a time as any," I said, sitting down on one of the chairs that surrounded the large fire pit. "Besides, he'd be more pissed if he came back here only to find you gone."

I offered her a beer when she sat down next to me, but she declined, shaking her head. "Not of legal drinking age, remember?"

I laughed and glanced over at Colt, who was standing on the other side, grinning. "We're not overly concerned with rules around these parts, *sweetheart*," I informed her.

She rolled her eyes and settled back in her chair, pulling her hair up in a messy bun. We sat in silence for a bit, just listening to the crackle of the fire and feeling the chilly air shifting through the desert night. I eyed her, drinking my beer. The firelight made her lightly tanned skin more bronzed, and the blue of her eyes seemed to glow in the darkness. She was dressed conservatively, and the tight jeans and loose-fitting sweater shouldn't have been a turn-on, but they were. I watched her face. The weariness and defeat in her posture, combined with the sadness and fear in her expression, spoke of someone who'd had a lot taken from her, but was still standing. Like she was still here, but not entirely sure why. I completely understood that, and it was strange relating to her on that level. I didn't like it. It made me think about my own past I'd resolved years ago. Or so I thought.

"What?" she asked, suddenly. She nervously fidgeted with the locket around her neck.

I was staring and not hiding it. It was clear she had no idea just how gorgeous she was. I shook my head and glanced away only to find Colt's questioning look. I downed my beer and tossed the empty bottle into the flames, the sound of the glass breaking making her jump a little. Colt gave a low, rumbling chuckle, but I cut him a look that just made him grin like the Cheshire Cat.

Then, we heard the rumble of a bike pulling up. Colt came to attention, and I stood up. "Looks like he's here."

If Kate had seemed freaked out before, that was nothing compared to how she looked now. She was physically shaking in her chair and looked like she was going to be sick.

"I don't know if I can do this," she whispered to herself. Her breaths were coming in and out quick, and she looked like she was either ready to run or pass out.

Before I realized what I was doing, I reached out and gently touched her shoulder. "He's not going to hurt you." I knew that much was true for a noncombatant. However, if anyone tried to harm his family and the club, all bets were off, no matter who you were.

"What the fuck is going on?" Viking boomed a couple of minutes later as he walked into the backyard with Wolf right behind him.

Viking could look scary as hell. Even at forty-nine years old, that guy was built like a brick shithouse. As soon as I saw him, I was hit with just how much Kate resembled him. They had the same blond hair, although he was starting to gray, and blue eyes, height, and facial features as well. It was almost eerie.

When no one answered him, he looked to me for an explanation.

"This is Kate." I glanced over to where she sat, frozen in the wooden chair. I turned my gaze back to my president. Viking must not have seen her when he first walked out here because he looked stunned to see someone besides Colt and me. "She came here looking for you."

"Why?" he asked, sounding marginally less angry than he had just a minute ago.

"I'll let her answer that. We'll head back in."

I followed Colt and Wolf inside but looked over my shoulder before the door closed behind me. Viking had a look on his face I rarely saw: confusion at the fact that three of his officers were leaving him out there alone with some unknown girl.

6

KATE

I watched as the guys walked back into the building. I only knew Wolf's name, which I assumed was another road name, whatever that meant, but he was the only one to introduce himself to me. The other one who had met me outside never told me his name, nor had the one from upstairs.

The man who apparently was my father stood staring down at me. His piercing gaze unnerved me, and I had no idea what was going on in his head. It was obvious he wasn't expecting someone like me to be the reason he was called to come back over here tonight.

I had practiced what I was going to say to him during my drive to Las Vegas, but all of that left my head the moment I laid eyes on him. I could see the similarities between us and I wondered if he did, too.

After a few silent moments, he sat down in the chair across from me.

"Mind telling me what's going on, darlin'?" he asked, his voice much softer than it had been when he came barreling into the backyard a few minutes ago.

His endearment caused tears to well in my eyes, even though I was sure it didn't mean anything. He probably called every woman darlin'. Still, I had to blink back the tears before I could start explaining what I was doing here.

"Um..." I started. I didn't know how to ease into a conversation like this, so I just blurted it out instead. "I think you're my father."

He went quiet again, looking at me so intensely I started to squirm a bit.

"Come again?"

"Well, my grandmother passed away a few weeks ago, and while I was going through her things, I found my birth certificate. It listed you as my father."

"Okay..."

I could tell he was trying to comprehend what I was telling him, but I was nervous, so I rambled on anyway.

"My mom never told me about you, and recently I learned she never told you about me, either. I'm sorry to show up like this, but I guess I was...curious."

More silence. I wasn't sure what to do, so I just sat there and let him take time to process what I'd just said.

"What's your mom's name?"

"Her name was Karen Nixon."

A brief flash of recognition crossed his face before he asked, "Was?"

"Uh, yeah. She died when I was six."

"Oh, I'm sorry," he replied and, surprisingly, his words sounded sincere.

"I apologize again for showing up like this. I'm not even sure why I came here." That was the truth, and now I was starting to feel awkward. I had zero expectations, and I knew not to get my hopes up about anything. If I did, I knew I'd end up being disappointed.

Besides, the craziness I saw in the club while I was waiting for him showed me my mother's concerns about telling him she was pregnant weren't completely unfounded. It definitely wasn't a place for a family. And yet, here I was. I didn't know what else to say, and I started to let my insecurities get the better of me, so I decided it was time for me to leave.

"I think...maybe I should go," I said, haltingly. "And...if you want to, we can talk tomorrow. Or later, or whenever..."

"Do you live nearby?" he asked as I stood to walk away.

"I'm staying in Vegas for the time being, but I don't know if it's a permanent move or not," I answered.

Viking considered me for a long moment. I cleared my throat to move things along, since I didn't want to be standing out here all night in the cold. "Sorry, you've got me at a loss, darlin'. I wasn't expecting this when the guys called me." He paused, standing up. "How 'bout you leave me your number and we meet up tomorrow or the next day to talk some more?"

He handed me his cell phone, and I programmed my number

into it. That gesture filled me with a little hope, knowing he wasn't rejecting me right off the bat.

"That sounds good," I said as I started walking with him back to the clubhouse. "I look forward to hearing from you."

He quickly ushered me through the building, both of us ignoring the curious stares thrown our way. When we reached my car, he opened the door for me. As I sat down, I looked up at him. The light coming off the building shined down on him, and I realized we looked even more alike than I had previously thought.

I think he noticed the same thing because I could see him studying me with a smile on his face. "It was nice meeting you, Kate. I'll talk to you soon."

"You too, Viking." The name sounded odd to me, but his grin showed he was good with me calling him that. He closed my car door and went back inside.

I didn't know what the future held, but I grabbed on to a small sliver of hope that maybe some sort of relationship could be formed with Viking. I had to believe that after what'd happened lately, I finally might get the happiness I'd always wanted.

It had been a couple of days since my visit to the clubhouse. Viking and I had texted back and forth a bit, and he invited me to breakfast this morning. He was heading out of town for a few days and wanted to meet up before getting on the road.

From the moment I woke up, I could feel the butterflies fluttering around in my stomach. Every man in my life, up to this point, had rejected me, verbally abused me, or just plain disappointed me. I wanted to believe, more than anything, that Viking was different, but I was afraid history would repeat itself. I told myself not to get my hopes up and expect anything different this time around.

After I dressed warmly, I headed to the restaurant thirty minutes earlier than our planned meeting, unable to sit around my dingy room any longer. I could only afford to stay at a rundown motel. It was pretty sketchy during the day and downright frightening at night. It was about fifteen minutes outside of Las Vegas, and Viking lived another twenty minutes further than that. Since I didn't know the area very well, we were meeting at a retro diner in his neighborhood.

I glanced at the "Help Wanted" sign taped to the window as I walked in and was immediately greeted by a middle-aged woman wearing a blue dress with white pinstripes, a frilly apron, and matching headband. Her uniform looked like it was straight out of an old-school movie, but she had a kindness in her eyes that I was immediately drawn to.

"Table for one?" she asked with no judgment in her tone.

"Actually, I'm meeting someone. I can wait at the counter."

"Don't be silly. You can have that booth over there." She motioned with the coffee pot she was holding.

I looked in the direction she was pointing and saw a round booth and made my way over to it. The diner wasn't too full. There was music playing softly above, and I had to stop myself from checking the time on my phone every few seconds. A few moments later, she came over and left a couple of menus in the center of the table.

"Can I get you something to drink?"

I glanced quickly at her nametag. "Coffee would be great. Thanks, Pam."

My nerves hadn't allowed me to sleep well last night and I was in desperate need of some caffeine. After another refill, I heard some motorcycles as they pulled into the parking lot. I looked out my window, squinting against a bright Nevada sun. Several men on bikes parked along the street, at a slight angle in a neat row. They moved in tandem, smoothly and almost gracefully, like they were in tune with each other. I recognized Viking and a couple of others. He'd mentioned a few guys from his club were leaving with him, but I was still surprised they were here, too.

I had been intimidated by them at the clubhouse, but based on what I'd seen so far, I knew if I wanted to see my father, I needed to get used to seeing them as well.

My mind flashed back to the guy who had come outside to question me when I first showed up at the clubhouse. I still didn't know his name. I hadn't realized they all had a patch with their name on it until Wolf had introduced himself. Once I saw the mystery guy again there was too much going on that I'd forgotten to look.

Even though I didn't know his name, I couldn't forget how attractive he was. I don't recall ever meeting someone who looked like him before. He had light-brown hair and blue eyes that looked almost gray. Under his leather vest, he had worn a fitted T-shirt that showed off the various tattoos on his toned arms. He was almost *too* gorgeous, but he had a hard edge to him that both intrigued me and scared me a little. It was a heady combination, and I found myself thinking about him more than a few times over the last couple of days. I wasn't sure if I was hoping he would be here this morning or not.

I shook my head, trying to clear it of all thoughts of the mystery man. I was here to get to know my father.

On cue, I heard the bell above the door ding and watched as Viking walked in, followed by Wolf, Mystery Guy, the guy who had been tending bar at the party, and another guy I didn't recognize. Everybody in the restaurant paused what they were doing and glanced at the front door before going back to their food. It appeared they were regulars when they all said a friendly hello to Pam. Viking scanned the restaurant before noticing me in the back corner. The other guys moved to a table on the other side of the restaurant, and my father headed my way.

"Hey there." Viking was a huge, scary-looking biker, but right now, he looked to be just as nervous as I was. "Do you mind if I sit there?" he asked while pointing to where I was sitting on the far side of the table with my back against the wall. "I like sitting where I can see everything," he explained.

It seemed odd to me, but I went ahead and moved to the other side of the booth.

Once he was settled, Pam came to take our order. We both chose the biscuits and gravy, and I chuckled about us picking the same thing. It seemed silly, but I enjoyed knowing we liked the same food.

"Thanks for meeting like this. I don't know how long this trip is going to take and I didn't want you to think I was avoiding you."

He was definitely perceptive because that's exactly what I would've thought if I didn't hear from him.

"I also wanted to invite you out to the house to meet Meredith and the boys. This trip is urgent, but we'll make plans for you to come over as soon as I'm back," he continued.

From our text messages, I knew Meredith was his wife, and he had twin sons, Finn and Gunnar, who had just turned thirteen.

"You want me to meet your family?" I wasn't expecting that, and I was positive the uncertainty was evident in my voice.

"Of course. You're my daughter. Why wouldn't you meet them?"

It was a shock to me he actually believed what I was telling him. I knew I had no reason to lie, but *he* didn't know that. Never would I have thought he'd accept my announcement, no questions asked.

"You're not going to take a paternity test or anything to prove that I'm your daughter?" I had no idea why I was questioning him. I should have been happy, but this seemed too good to be true.

"Do you have any reason to lie to me?"

"Well, no."

"Kate, when you told me who your mother was I knew there was a possibility you were my daughter. You told me your birthday the other day, and it matches up with the dates I was with Karen. And if I needed any further proof, you look exactly like my younger sister, Anneliese. I noticed it the night we met, but I was too stunned to say anything."

I let out a breath I didn't realize I was holding. He believed me, and he wasn't sending me away.

"I don't know what you were expecting when you came looking for me, but I don't turn my back on family," he said, sounding genuine, and looking me right in the eyes as he spoke. "I'm happy to have you here, and when I get back, I plan on catching up."

I couldn't hold back the couple of tears that ran down my cheeks. "Thank you." Those words were the only ones I could get out while wiping at my face.

I was sure I was making him uncomfortable with my emotional response, so I excused myself to the restroom, so I could freshen up.

As I walked across the restaurant, I had to pass the table where the other guys were sitting. I was a couple of tables away when I glanced up and my eyes locked with those belonging to Mr. Handsome. He wasn't smiling, but he wasn't frowning at me either. The way he was looking at me was like I was the only thing he saw in this whole place, and it made my face heat up. Self-conscious, I quickly looked down to avoid his gaze and noticed the patch telling me his name was Mac.

I took a few minutes in the bathroom to collect myself. Between the conversation with Viking and being distracted by Mac, I was a mess. I fixed my hair and touched up my makeup before I decided to head back out. I didn't make eye contact with any of the Desert Sinners as I rushed past their table and back to my seat.

My food was waiting for me and eating helped fill in some of the awkward silence and glances. While Viking seemed more at ease than me, it was clear he was still trying to get used to the idea of me being his daughter. It made me less anxious knowing he was nervous, too.

"So..." I started, deciding to try to learn a little bit more about the man sitting across from me, "how long have you been with the...um, with the club?"

He smiled, seemingly pleased by my question. "Over twenty-five years," he answered, with immense pride. "Started it way back with two brothers of mine before Vegas got to be as crazy as it is."

"Wow..." I poked at my biscuit. "Why'd you start a club?"

He laughed out loud. "I'm not meant for a nine-to-five job and the crap that goes with it. I needed something where I felt free. Where I could do my own thing. Falcon and Rome felt the same way."

I tried to digest what that meant, then the other night's antics and what I'd read in the news came into my mind. "You mean...like doing illegal stuff?"

Viking's amusement cooled a bit. "Me and those that are part of the club choose to live a way of life that many may not agree with. And we won't apologize for making our own way in this world." His expression became serious. "Kate, darlin'," he said, his voice soothing and compelling, "you have to understand that your mom had a good reason to keep you shielded from me and who I am. I don't agree with it, since I don't like knowing I had family out there I couldn't protect and take care of. But I understand, and what's done is done. Know that I fully accept you, and I wouldn't say it unless I meant it. My family is your family. The club is your family, but there are rules you'll have to learn and decide if you want to live by. It's your choice, but once you accept, you accept all of it. All of us, as we are. Or not at all. Do you understand?"

I swallowed, my throat as dry as the biscuit. "And if I don't?"

He sighed. "You'll always be part of my family—Meredith, me, and the boys—that goes without saying," he said, carefully. "But I'd rather have you be part of the club as well. It's the other major thing in my life, other than my wife and kids, including you. Not sharing that part of me with you...it wouldn't be easy, Kate, but it's possible."

I gnawed on my lip, trying to process everything. I appreciated his honesty and trust that I could handle whatever he threw at me. But it was all so heavy. I inhaled and exhaled loudly and met his gaze. "I'll try," I said. "That's all I can promise."

He gave a nod and dug into his food. We didn't talk much after that, which I was okay with. He always answered my questions, no matter how personal they got, but so far, he hadn't said anything about me ignoring the questions about myself and my past he had asked when we were texting. I knew, at some point, I'd have to open up, and that ate at me more than anything else. I'd never opened up to anyone. I never had anyone who cared to know, but even after such a short time, Viking wanted to know everything about me, even the silly stuff, like what my favorite food was or asking how my day was. Simple, but oh so wonderful. And still too good to be true.

"Are you going to stay for a bit?" he asked when I didn't get up at the same time he did.

"Yeah, I need a little more caffeine before I do anything else."

"Okay, I'll see you soon," he said, squeezing my shoulder briefly. Then he headed to the front to pay for our meal.

I watched the four other guys follow Viking out of the restaurant and climb on their bikes. Through the window, I could feel Mac's eyes on me, even though they were hidden behind his sunglasses, and I felt my whole body flush. The sound of their roaring engines was starting to become familiar, and almost comforting.

A couple of minutes later, Pam came back over to offer me a refill on my coffee.

"I wasn't expecting a group of Desert Sinners to join you when you said you were waiting for someone." The smile on her face told me she wasn't speaking negatively about them, just surprised.

"Do you know them?"

"Honey, everyone around here knows them." Now I was curious, so I waited for her to continue. "They don't have the best reputation and often clash with our local police, but I've never had a problem with any of them. And they always tip well," she added with a little wink.

Her description of the club gave me pause. I still wasn't sure how I felt about hanging out with a motorcycle club with a less than stellar reputation, but it wasn't enough to discourage me from getting to know my father. And what he'd said earlier really had an impact on me.

"So, what's a nice girl like you hanging out with them, anyway?" Pam asked, not hiding her interest.

"Viking…he's, um, my father. We both just found out."

"Oh! So, you're like an MC princess." She said that like it was a good thing.

"Nothing like that, more like a lost girl just trying to find her way."

I had no idea why I was so open with Pam. Maybe it was the motherly way she had about her, something that had been absent from my life for some time.

As she started clearing our plates from the table, an idea hit me. And with that idea came the decision that I was going to stay and make this work with Viking and my new family. I pointed to the window. "I noticed there was a help wanted sign in the window. You still looking for someone?"

"I think we could work something out." She smiled at me. "Why don't you come back later to talk to my manager?"

"I'll be there," I said, smiling genuinely for the first time in ages, and with a sense that everything was going to be okay.

7

MAC

The last few days had been tough. The Phantoms were causing more problems and were determined to use our routes for their own smuggling activities. It was bad enough they were trying to move in on our territory, selling their drugs and weapons, but the Phantoms were also known to be actively involved in human trafficking. That was not our thing, and we didn't tolerate others conducting that, or any other kind of business, on our own turf. Our last run had been successful, and we now had a new client who was going to need regular shipments of guns. We'd also ensured the routes between us and Reno, as well as Los Angeles, were still holding strong.

We had just finished up church when Viking asked the officers in attendance to stay behind. "While we were gone, I had one of our guys look into Kate," he announced as soon as the door closed.

"Doubting her story about you being the daddy?" I chuckled, the others joining in.

"No, asshole," Viking growled in a low voice but continued, "I wasn't lying when I said she looked just like Anneliese. But I was curious about where she was living and why she was suddenly in Vegas. She hasn't shared much about her past."

I knew Viking and Kate had been keeping in contact, but I wondered what was making her so guarded. Granted, she was probably still grieving. She'd just moved from California to Vegas, and it'd only been a week, but Viking was the type that when he decided something, he was all in.

"What did they find?" Wolf asked.

"She's started working at the diner nearby, so it sounds like she plans on staying put, at least for now. But she's been living in some rundown piece of shit motel, in a part of Vegas we don't have much control over. I want to ask her to stay with me and Meredith, but I don't want to scare her off. We all know, with the Phantoms running around, she would be safer somewhere I could keep an eye on her."

"Do we know where she came from?" That was another question from Wolf.

He seemed overly curious about Kate, but Viking wouldn't take kindly to anyone trying to get with his newfound daughter.

"She was living with her grandmother before she passed away not too long ago. She has an uncle back in Apple Valley, but there's something you need to know about him," he said grimly. "Her uncle, Stuart, tried to patch into this club years ago, when we were a relatively new MC. That's how I met her mom. Her uncle was a dick. He was more interested in the image that came with our lifestyle than actually living by our code. He didn't even make it to a vote. Had to physically kick him out when he refused to leave."

That instantly put me on alert. It explained a lot about her behavior.

Viking continued, his expression hard. "He had to have known I was her father. I'm guessing him not telling me was his way of getting back at the club. I'll deal with that, but I asked you guys to stay back because I want you to watch out for her. She's out there struggling, and I want to help her, but with the crap going on with the Phantoms, I don't want them catching wind of the fact that I have a daughter."

"Got it," we all agreed.

We may not be upstanding citizens, but we didn't allow anything to happen to each other or our families.

"Since I'm too obvious a target and might draw unnecessary attention, Wolf, I want you to drive by her place tomorrow and check it out as well as the surrounding area. Until people know she's under the protection of the Desert Sinners, she's fair game for anyone. Be discreet."

"Yes, sir," Wolf said.

We stood up to leave, but Viking stopped me, letting the others exit. Wolf gave me a raised-brow look before I closed the door in his face. "Yeah, Prez?" I asked, turning around to face Viking. He was leaning over the table, and I knew something heavy was on his mind. I didn't interrupt his thought; I just waited until he was ready to say something.

"I think we've both figured out that Kate's life has been...as far as we know...sheltered." He paused, standing tall. "She has no idea what this life is about. I can tell her home life was hard, and having an asshole uncle probably didn't help. I think that's why she's here…to escape. But I also know she's earnest in wanting a relationship with me, and that has to include the club as well." He stepped away from the desk and faced the window that looked out over the front courtyard, folding his arms across his chest. I watched his intense reflection in the glass. "You're the first person she met, so that might help."

I ran a hand over my scalp. "What are you asking, Viking?"

"I need you to help her. I can only do so much on my end. Get her comfortable with the club, but don't rush her. I'm trusting you to keep her safe, personally." He looked over his shoulder at me. "No one touches her, Mac, *no one*. Go with Wolf tomorrow to check on her, then start spending some time with her. Show her who we really are at our core."

"And the less prettier side of the club?" I asked.

Viking sighed, glancing out the window again. "One hurdle at a time, brother."

"You got it." I turned and walked out, closing the door behind me. I stood there for a minute, dissecting our conversation. Christ, my president wanted me to befriend his gorgeous daughter with the understanding that befriending her was all I could do.

The stress from the shit with the Phantoms was already

getting to me, and now I had this Kate situation to deal with. I knew the perfect remedy would be finding a chick to sink my dick into. Unfortunately, each time I thought of who I wanted, an image of a certain blonde popped into my head. I was fucked, and not in a good way.

8

KATE

The loud banging—and not the bright, late morning sun—woke me up, just as it had every day this week. It seemed the couple renting out the room next to mine had a habit of kicking each other out on a regular basis. This resulted in one of them banging on the door repeatedly until the other finally let them back in, or the cops came by to break it up.

The first time it happened, I called the clerk at the front desk, who laughed off my complaint and never did anything about it. Between them and the other residents who apparently stayed awake all night, I hadn't gotten a decent night's sleep since I got here. I needed to find a new place to live since I planned on staying in Vegas for the foreseeable future. I was starting to get more steady hours at the diner, but it was going to be a while before I had enough saved up to move out of here.

Knowing I wouldn't be able to fall back asleep, I decided to shower and get ready for the day. I was going to meet my coworker, Evelyn, for an early lunch; otherwise, I didn't have any other plans for my day off. I slipped on the pair of flip-flops I kept next to the bed since I refused to walk on the carpet barefoot. I grabbed a pair of yoga pants and a tank top out of the rickety old dresser and headed to the bathroom. The lighting in here filled the room with a harsh yellow glow, the water pressure in the shower barely produced more than a trickle, and the towels were the roughest pieces of fabric I ever felt. But this was all my budget would allow.

After I quickly washed up, brushed my hair, and put on a touch of makeup, I heard the unmistakable sound of motorcycle engines outside.

I peeked out at the parking lot from behind the heavy drapes, and immediately recognized Wolf and Mac. Mac was climbing off his bike, but Wolf's bike was still running. They were talking, but I couldn't hear anything from here.

No one knew I was here, not even Viking, despite the fact he'd asked a few times. Were they here to conduct some sort of illegal transaction? It wouldn't be the first time I saw a drug deal go down in the parking lot.

The text alert going off on my phone shook me out of my reverie, and I let the blinds close in front of me. Picking my phone up from the bedside table, I made a face when I saw it was Jonathan...again.

Jonathan: *Please talk to me. I miss you.*

I'd tried to talk to him once since I left but he made a bunch of excuses for his behavior, and he didn't take any responsibility for the hurtful things he'd said. I explained to him that I thought it was best if we took a break from contacting each other for a while, but he was relentless. I thought about blocking him, but I didn't want to completely cut him off yet. Our friendship was hanging on by a thread, but I wanted to give him the chance to fix things...eventually. I just wasn't ready to fix things now.

I threw the phone on the bed and grabbed my shoes so I could finish getting dressed. I had just finished tying them when I heard a knock at the door. I immediately tensed, not saying anything, hoping the person would go away.

"Kate, open up. We saw you looking out the window."

I recognized Mac's voice right away. I hadn't seen him or the other members since breakfast at the diner with Viking. Fear washed over me, and I wondered if something happened to Viking. I'd just met the man but the thought of something happening to him before I even got to know him made me feel like I was losing something special all over again.

"Is everything okay?" I asked before I opened the door all the way.

When I looked out, Mac's eyes slammed into mine. He had a way about him that was a little too intense for me, like now, and I wasn't sure if it was a turn-on or a turn-off. Right now, a little bit of both.

"Everything's fine," he said softly. I blushed when his eyes roved over me from head to toe. I didn't dress like the girls at their club, but he seemed to approve of my jeans and long-sleeved top.

"Where's Wolf?" I asked, for lack of words.

His eyes narrowed. "Why do you care?"

I stared back at him. "I saw you both outside; just being polite in asking," I shot back, feeling bold. I was done with men treating me like crap, but I knew it was dangerous to finally find my nerve with a badass biker like Mac. "What are you two even doing here? No one knows I'm here."

"There's not a lot we don't know when it comes to what's happening in our city, sweetheart."

Ugh, I thought, *not that word again*. When Mac grinned, I realized I must have said it aloud. I blushed. "No, seriously, why are you here?" I asked, going for civility.

He shrugged, his focus never leaving my face, like he was trying to capture every feature and commit it to memory. "You're new to Vegas, and we protect what's ours."

I shivered because instinctively I knew Mac meant every syllable that came from his mouth. "I don't belong to anyone, Mac."

"That's where you're wrong, Kate." He stepped in, and I stepped back. "You'll realize that, and you'll even appreciate it when you're finally one of us."

I should have been scared at the idea of being "part of a biker gang," but the idea of being part of something, of knowing that someone had my back—and I knew both Mac and Viking meant it as both a promise and a creed—made my chest go tight at how absolute it felt. It was confusing but uplifting as well.

Wordlessly, my whole body shaking, I turned around to grab my purse but spun back when I heard the door close. Mac was moving around my room, like he had the right to do so. All he did was make the space seem even smaller. Mac was around six foot, and in normal circumstances he was intimidating, but right now, I felt like the room was closing in on me. My pulse sped up, and I didn't know if my body was warning me to flee or if I was reacting to being stuck in a room with an incredibly good-looking man. I could feel my palms starting to sweat and my breathing quicken.

"Relax, babe, I'm not going to hurt you." Mac's soothing tone was almost convincing, but his burning gaze ramped up my nerves again. I realized the tension wasn't one of violence, but rather somewhat sexual. I wondered if he looked at every woman like that.

I cleared my throat, checking the contents of my purse to give my hands something to do and to distract my mind from unnerving thoughts of Mac. "Well, you saw me, you can report back to Viking that I'm alive and breathing."

Mac smiled, a nice one that was disarming as hell. "Are you working today?" he asked as I grabbed my keys from my nightstand.

"Nope, got the day off. But I'm meeting a friend for lunch, and I'm going to be late if I don't leave soon."

"A friend?" He frowned. "Who?"

"Not that it's any of your business, but yes, a friend. Evelyn and I work together at the diner."

I couldn't figure out why he was grilling me about what I

was doing today. "This your phone?" Mac asked, picking up my beat-up cell phone that was still on my bed. It drew him even closer into my personal space. This close up, he was even more attractive. I could smell hints of leather and smoke, but also an earthy, desert fresh scent over that.

"Yes. Why?" I asked, my throat dry.

"I want to give you my number, in case you need me for anything," he stated casually, programming his number in my phone, his own buzzing a few seconds later.

Those last words reverberated in my skull: *In case you need me for anything.*

"I don't need anything from anybody," I stated, softly.

He smiled again, this time, not so nicely. "Just remember this one thing, Kate. Anything you need, I'll be there. Whenever you want me, I won't hesitate."

The heat in his voice slithered through my veins like molten lava. Speechless, I could feel my whole face get blazing hot again at his innuendo, something Mac always managed to do at least once when we saw each other, which was rare, and probably a good thing or I would have burned up into ash by now.

"Good seeing you, sweetheart," Mac said as he opened the door and, without a backward glance, left.

I stood there like an idiot, still processing everything and my heart racing fast in my chest. I was hot all over, and my brain was mush.

It was cowardly, but I waited to leave my room until I knew Mac was gone and I'd calmed down. Once I sat behind the driver's seat of my car, I reflected on our interaction that had just occurred. I couldn't focus on anything other than the way Mac looked at me during our conversation.

I didn't know what it signaled, only that something had happened. His words kept playing over and over in my head the whole car ride to the Strip, where I was meeting Evelyn, and I couldn't shake this idea that Mac and me...well...there was definitely something to be worked out between us. And I wasn't sure whether to be excited or worried.

9

MAC

"Want to grab some lunch?" Viper asked from somewhere above me.

I slid out from under the car I was working on, which was taking a lot longer to fix than it should have. I kept thinking about a hot blonde I had no right to think about—not to mention the dirtier thoughts that Viking would kill me over—and it was pissing me off I was letting some girl distract me so much.

She's not just some girl.

"Yo, Mac, hello?" Viper said, knocking on the side of the car.

"Yeah. Sure. Give me five minutes." I stood up to head to the back room so I could get cleaned up a bit.

When I walked in, I saw Wolf sitting at one of the tables, typing away furiously on his phone.

"What's up?" I asked when he put his phone back down.

"Don't know, man. Hawk and Fitz said they've come across some weird shit on their ride up to Reno."

Hawk was Wolf's brother, and Fitz was our Sergeant-at-Arms. The two of them left a couple of days ago to make sure our charter club there was on the lookout for anything having to do with the Phantoms.

The Desert Sinners had started in Las Vegas, but over the years, several charters popped up all around the southwest. It gave us strength in numbers but also put a target on our backs with the Phantoms. They figured if they could get rid of us, they could control our allies and would also gain a considerable area.

"What kind of weird shit?" I asked as I scrubbed my hands, trying to get rid of the grease all over them.

"They checked on a few of our clients who were suddenly hesitant to do business with us. Hawk didn't push too hard for details, but it was obvious the Phantoms had paid them a visit."

This shit with the Phantoms was getting worse, and if we didn't act carefully, it was going to end up with a full-blown war between the two clubs.

"When are they coming back?"

"In a couple of days. Viking has them checking on a few more things before they head home."

I nodded in response. It sounded like Viking had everything under control, which wasn't surprising. However, I knew it was only a matter of time before we were dealing with this more aggressively. No doubt they'd be our main topic at church.

"Viper and I are headed to lunch. Want to go?" I asked, tossing my paper towels in the trash.

"Food sounds good. We eating at the diner?" The asshole had a shit-eating grin when he asked that.

Not taking the bait, I merely nodded my head and walked out. No way I was going to give him the satisfaction of knowing that's exactly where I wanted to go. He'd been on me since we stopped by the shit-ass motel Kate was staying at. And the fact that I'd been eating at the diner at least once a day since then. I knew he saw the way I looked at her while she worked, but I wasn't going to acknowledge his comments about it. I was doing what Viking asked, that was it. So what if I enjoyed looking at her while doing what I was ordered to do? I wasn't the only one who liked to look though, and that irritated the fuck out of me. I was not the guy that got crazy about some girl, but this one had me all tied up in knots.

The three of us walked the few blocks to the restaurant, and I immediately spotted Kate's car in the parking lot. While I wouldn't share my personal thoughts with Wolf, I couldn't lie to myself. I was excited at the possibility of seeing her.

"Colt's gonna join us in a few minutes," Viper said as he opened the door.

As soon as I stepped in, I saw Kate. It wasn't bad enough I had a hard time keeping my eyes off her, but now she was standing up on her toes reaching for something on the shelf above her head. Her dress was rising up, exposing the back of her thighs. Just a little bit more and we would all have a clear shot of her ass.

"Well, that's a mighty fine view," Wolf drawled.

I gave him a warning look. "Knock it off, asshole."

His responding laugh got the attention of the gorgeous waitress.

"Oh, hey guys! Table for three?" Kate asked as she walked over to us, a massive grin on her face.

"Actually, there'll be four of us. Colt's on his way," Viper explained, as she grabbed some menus and led us to the table in the back that we preferred.

She took our drink order and walked away. My eyes never left her until she rounded the corner.

I turned back to the table and saw Viper watching me with a raised brow. I decided to ignore his questioning glance. Viking had asked me and Wolf to be discreet, and here I was, being obvious as fuck.

"What's up?" Colt asked as he joined our group.

"Not much. Just appears Mac here has a little crush on Viking's daughter," Viper decided to announce.

Wolf started laughing hysterically while Colt just looked at me with a small smile. I flipped them all off and went back to reading my menu.

"You know you can't fuck her, right?" Colt asked after he sat down across from me. Leave it up to him to turn this into a serious discussion.

"I'm not going to fuck her. She has a nice ass, that's it." The conversation needed to end before she came back and heard us.

"Did you guys check out where she was staying?" Viper asked, as we all looked over the menu and decided what we wanted to eat.

"It was a total shithole. The whole area is bad, man. Viking needs to get her the hell out of there," Wolf answered with a frown.

I agreed. I hated the thought of her staying there unprotected. When we'd reported back to Viking, he assured us he had a plan, but he had to go about it in a way that wouldn't scare her off. Kate seeing members of the club nearly every day was helping her get used to us. She wasn't ready to participate or even witness another wild party night, but I thought she might be up for one of our more relaxed family barbecues that Meredith spearheaded every month at the clubhouse.

A few minutes later, Kate came back to take our order. It was quiet in the diner, only an older couple on the other side of the restaurant was here, so we convinced Kate to take a break and join us when she brought out our food. She always declined but not today, which pleased all of us. It meant her comfort level with the club, and us, was heading in a positive direction.

"How do you like it out here so far?" Viper asked Kate when she pulled up a chair and sat at the end of the table.

Even though Viper was always looking for his next hookup, I knew he wasn't hitting on her. He seemed genuinely interested in what was going on with her, and, like all of us, I knew that stemmed from the respect he had for Viking.

"It's actually better than I expected," she replied, glancing up briefly and looking right at me.

"You plan on sticking around for a while?" This was from Wolf, and unlike Viper, I knew he would flirt with her given a chance. I gripped my fork a little harder than necessary as I awaited her answer.

"I… I'm really not sure."

"I think Viking would be disappointed if you left," I added.

Her smile was bright at the mention of her father.

We continued to chat until her break was over and it was time for us to head back to the shop.

As we walked out the door, I turned back around to look at Kate once more. She gave me a shy smile and then ducked her head and went back to work.

I left there knowing I wanted her to stay, but not sure what that meant. And knowing I couldn't break Viking's trust, no matter how much I wanted her.

10

KATE

I couldn't think of a time I'd ever been this nervous. Viking had invited me over to his house for dinner tonight, where I was going to meet his wife, Meredith, for the first time, as well as his sons, my half-brothers.

The last week had been a calm one, and I was getting into a regular routine. I saw Mac, usually with Wolf, almost every day. I took my breaks with the boys, and while our conversations weren't deep or personal, Mac always asked how I was doing and if I needed anything. The *way* he'd ask if I needed anything made me blush every time, and Mac would smile that slow, knowing smile.

And when I was working, when his lunch hour stretched to another hour, I always felt his eyes on me the whole time. It should have weirded me out, but it didn't. When Jonathan would openly stare at me, with *that* look in his eyes, it'd been a huge turn-off, but with Mac, it was a major turn-*on*. It made no sense, it just felt…good.

Today, at lunch, when I'd blurted to him about tonight, he told me to have fun, be myself, and say whatever was on my mind. Simple but well-meaning. I could almost forget the darker, seedier side to him and the club, but I knew I'd have to deal with that at some point, just not right this moment.

My car was parked in the driveway of a large, modern-style home, and had been for the past ten minutes. It was not at all the house I thought a biker would live in. The rooflines were all different heights, the windows all different shapes, and the red brick façade on the lower half of the house was a nice contrast to the cream-colored paint. The landscaping was beautiful, there was a small, lush patch of grass, and the rest was a mix of rocks and succulents.

Inside the house was my newfound family and it was all a little overwhelming. I never had a problem with the fact that I was an only child, but I always wondered what it would have been like to grow up with siblings. Now that I had the chance to be a part of a real family, all of my fears came rushing back. What if they hated me? What if they were pissed I'd appeared out of nowhere and disrupted their dynamic?

I was so lost in my head, I didn't notice someone walking out of the house.

"Everything okay out here?" A beautiful brunette with bright emerald eyes asked through my slightly open window.

"Um, yeah, everything's fine," I replied as I turned off my car and got out. "You must be Meredith." I stuck my hand out for her to shake.

"And you must be Kate." She smiled at me when she took my hand, and her kindness put me at ease. Maybe this wouldn't be as awkward as I'd imagined it. "Welcome."

I started to follow her back up to the house but then remembered something.

"Oh, wait," I said as I went back to my car and opened the back door. "Can't forget this." I held up the chocolate pie I'd picked up at the diner on my way over.

"That looks great!" Meredith said, smiling. "Viking has a bit of a sweet tooth, so you'll make him a happy man when he sees this."

We walked into the house, and I was just as shocked by the inside as I was by the outside. The front entry led into a large, open living area where three cream-colored couches surrounded a dark coffee table. Off to the right was a dining room, large enough to hold several people. Most everything was done in neutral colors with just small pops of color. I loved it.

"Viking's in the kitchen. We can go sit in there while he finishes up dinner."

"Okay." I followed Meredith into the kitchen, which was nothing short of a chef's dream. The large island took up the center of the room with state-of-the-art stainless steel appliances all along the walls.

"Wow!" I realized I said that out loud when both my father and Meredith chuckled.

"What can I say? I love to cook."

I laughed at his response, setting the pie on the counter. Cooking was the last thing I expected Viking to be into. But now that I was here, I couldn't wait to try whatever he was making for us.

"I'm glad you were able to make it tonight," he said, as he took a quick peek in the oven. He looked so relaxed in his blue jeans and a black T-shirt. He leaned back against the countertop with his massive arms crossed over his chest, a simple smile on his face.

"Me too," I replied, taking a seat at the breakfast bar.

And I was really happy to be here. As much as my grand-mother tried to show me love, I never felt like I was a part of a family. How could I, when the men of the house constantly reminded me how unwanted I was.

This was different than anything I had ever experienced, and I could feel my chest getting tight from the emotions it was invoking in me.

"Is she here yet?" I heard someone yell from down the hall-way. My feelings were getting too intense, so I was grateful for the interruption.

Before anyone could answer, two tornadoes, one blond and one brunette, came tearing through the kitchen.

"Boys! Be careful," Meredith reprimanded from her seat next to me.

Viking playfully caught them both by the collar of their shirts and turned them around to face me. "Guys, I want you to meet Kate, your sister." They both looked at me with a little question in their eyes. "Kate, this is Gunnar," Viking said as he pushed the blond forward a little bit. "And this is Finn." He did the same with the brunette.

"Hi there. Nice to meet you."

It was weird, but I could see the resemblances between all of us. I hadn't looked like my mom's side of the family at all, and now I was in a room with three other people that clearly looked like me.

"Is dinner ready yet?" Gunnar asked, and I found it funny that while I sat here feeling all sorts of emotions about my newfound family, he could only think about food. Seemed about right for a thirteen-year-old boy, and it relaxed me that this was being treated just like any other day. As emotional as this was for me, I was glad no one was making a huge deal over it, or me.

"A few more minutes," Meredith replied. "Why don't you guys go set the table?"

They grumbled a response but did as their mom asked.

The five of us enjoyed a dinner of the most delicious roasted chicken I'd ever eaten, along with bacon-wrapped asparagus, and homemade rolls. Everything was perfect.

Throughout dinner, the boys talked about school, sports, video games, and other teenaged boy topics at nonstop speeds. All I could do was listen and laugh at their antics and family stories. Meredith and Viking clearly loved their boys fiercely. It hurt a little that I never got to have that when I was a kid, but I was happy I got to have my own version of it now.

We had just finished the chocolate pie, which Viking thanked me several times for bringing, and moved into the living room for coffee. The boys headed up to their rooms so they could finish their homework and get ready for bed, since it was a school night.

We continued to chat about everything. I learned that the Desert Sinners owned a few local businesses, including an auto repair shop, a bar, and much to my embarrassment, a strip club. All of the members had jobs, most of them at a club-owned business. Even Meredith worked at the auto shop as the office manager.

Viking and Mac had both repeatedly told me they all took care of each other and worked hard to do so. To know they stood by their word with actions was profound to me. They trusted each other and respected each other to handle it. Trust was hard for me, but one of the walls I'd built to protect myself was starting to crack. I *knew* in my heart I could trust Viking, and if him, maybe Mac, too. Maybe, eventually, everyone in the club too.

I watched Meredith and my father talk, teasing each other as they told stories. They were affectionate and not afraid of showing it. To think, if we'd known about each other when I was a child... I pushed that aside because it'd do no good. I lived in the here and now, and I felt a sense of warmth and relief in having this second chance.

As the night went on, I could tell Viking wanted to say something but was trying to figure out how to bring it up. I saw him glance at Meredith, who gave him an almost imperceptible nod.

"So, I wanted to be honest with you about a couple of things," he said, leaning forward, resting his elbows on his thighs, his hands folded clasped together between his knees.

"First off, I know where you were living before you moved out here, and who you were living with."

I tensed, wondering if this was the moment the other shoe dropped. "How…?"

"Background check," he answered. "It's standard practice."

I exhaled, trying to relax. I didn't know how I felt about it, but I wasn't surprised. It made sense with their motto of protecting the club. I also knew I hadn't exactly opened up to Viking in the way he had but I needed more time, and he seemed to be all right with it. For now.

"Okay…I think I understand."

He watched my face a beat before he said, "Your uncle has a history with the Desert Sinners."

"*What?*" I knew Stu had lived in Las Vegas for a while, but I would never have guessed he had any dealings with a motorcycle club. In fact, he talked a lot of shit about people who owned motorcycles and always had something to say when he saw someone who was in a club.

"He actually tried to patch in a long time ago."

"Patch in?" I questioned.

"Become a member," Viking explained.

"Anyway, that's how I met Karen. Whatever your mother thought about me, I don't doubt your uncle kept you a secret just to spite me," he growled. It was clear he was angry about being left in the dark. "He knows I wouldn't have allowed him to have any part in raising you after your mom died."

I nodded in acknowledgment. Somehow, I knew that was

true. Viking was accepting of me now, and I was pretty sure he would have been twenty years ago.

"You said you had a couple of things you needed to be honest about?" I asked.

"I also wanted to let you know that I had a couple of my guys check in on you."

"Yeah, I figured…Mac stopped in and said hi," I said lamely, recalling the visit clearly, but Viking frowned. I quickly added, "Anyway, you were saying?"

"Right...anyway," he resumed. "You know the life I lead, the world we live in, isn't like what you're used to." He stopped, only continuing when I nodded my head in understanding. "We've got some shit going on with another club..." I started to interrupt, but he put his hand up to stop me. "Before you even ask, I'm not giving you any details on that. We don't share club business with our families."

I was starting to get freaked out. What kind of things were they involved in that their families couldn't know about? Maybe it'd been a bad idea to come here after all.

As quickly as that thought entered my head, I pushed it away. Even if they did some things I may not agree with, I couldn't deny that I'd been happier over the last couple of weeks getting to know Viking.

"That said, I don't like the fact that my daughter is living in a seedy motel, all alone and too far from us."

"It was all I could afford when I got into town. I'm going to start looking for a new place soon," I said, trying to reassure him. In fact, I'd already started saving for a deposit on an apartment near the diner and Viking's home. "I make pretty good tips at the diner, and Pam gives me as many hours as I'm willing to work."

"We have plenty of room here, Kate," Meredith piped up.

I looked at her, my mouth agape. Was she really asking me to move in with them? I thought it was a generous offer, but it was too soon for me.

"Oh, wow. That's nice…and unexpected. But I don't think I can accept. All of this is so new. It's just a little overwhelming." The truth was, I didn't want to do anything to disrupt how well things were going for me.

"That's understandable," Viking said, but I could tell he wasn't going to let this rest. "So, I have another proposition for you. There's a small, one-bedroom bungalow on the same property as the clubhouse, but it has its own entrance. You won't even see the guys from the club. It's nothing special, but you'd be doing me a favor if you stayed there."

"I'd be doing you a favor?" I asked, since I wasn't quite sure how that worked.

"Yeah, it needs a little bit of work. A good cleaning and some paint. If you could take care of that, I'd appreciate it."

Meredith reached over and grabbed my hand, squeezing tightly before releasing it. "Honestly, sweetie, Viking and I would sleep better at night knowing you're somewhere safe. Somewhere close by, in case you needed us."

I could feel my eyes watering at their kindness, but I managed to keep it together. "I…well…how much is the rent?" I asked, needing to make sure I could afford it before I accepted, and I definitely wanted to accept.

"We can talk about that later," he answered, and I had a feeling he wouldn't be bringing it up again. "So, what do you say? You want the place?"

I beamed at both him and Meredith. "Absolutely."

When I left that night, I had a true sense of home. I still needed to get to know my new family, and try to understand the club world, but I felt like it could and would happen. I was so happy I thought I'd burst. My life only seemed to get brighter, and as I looked up at the night sky, the billions of stars twinkling down at me, I gave a silent "thank you" to my mom. She'd promised in her last letter to me that she'd always look out for me. I was truly excited about my future. I just had to believe I deserved to be happy, and for the first time in my life, I felt anything was possible.

A few days later, as I did my hair and makeup, I thought about how moving to Vegas was the best thing I ever did. I was building a relationship with my father. His wife was super friendly and kind, and I'd enjoyed getting to know Finn and Gunnar.

I also loved my job at the diner. It was a grueling job with small pay, but working with Pam and Evelyn was fun. Pam had taken on a motherly role that I was so desperately missing, and Evelyn was turning out to be a great friend. She was even going out with me in a couple of weeks to celebrate my birthday.

Back in Apple Valley, everyone would always talk about

going to Vegas to celebrate their twenty-first birthday. I'd always wanted to make plans to do that but figured with my limited funds, it wouldn't happen. Now that I was living here, nothing was stopping me from having a fantastic birthday.

Viking, on the other hand, wasn't a huge fan of the idea when I'd told him at another family dinner the other night. He was taking his role as a father seriously. While I wanted to remind him I was an adult and was capable of handling things on my own, I was grateful that he cared enough to worry about me.

I heard my cell phone ring and smiled when I saw Viking's name.

"Hi there," I answered. I was still hesitant about calling him Dad. It seemed like that was something sacred, and I hadn't earned the right to do so yet.

"Hi, darlin'. Am I catching you at a bad time?"

"Nope, just getting ready for work," I answered as I searched my room for my work apron.

"Well, I wanted to make sure you were able to get this weekend off, so we can get you moved into your new place like we planned."

"I did, but I was hoping to come by today and see what all needs to be done."

"I'm leaving the keys with Mac at the clubhouse, if you want to come by tomorrow and check it out."

I hesitated, butterflies swarming in my stomach at the mention of Mac. The idea of seeing him again excited me. At the same time, I couldn't be lusting after someone Viking was close to, and I wasn't sure I was ready to get involved with a club member.

"Kate, honey, you there?"

"Uh, yeah, I'm here," I said quickly. "That works. Thank you. I don't have to be at work until three tomorrow afternoon. I'll come by on my way in."

"No problem. I'll talk to you soon."

"Bye," I responded, with a big, goofy smile on my face and looking forward to tomorrow for more than one reason.

11

MAC

I texted Kate that I'd be waiting outside her new place. There'd been a couple of other times I'd almost texted her but then thought better of it. I was supposed to be getting her used to the club, not developing anything else with her. But damn if she didn't consume my thoughts.

When Viking had made it known to the whole club that Kate would be living in the house on the other side of the property, no one had said anything but looks had been exchanged. She hadn't been formally introduced to the club yet, and that needed to be remedied quick. But to me, it was a no-brainer. Having her close by would make the job I'd been tasked with a lot easier. Plus, Meredith was working on introducing Kate soon.

I glanced over when I heard her car pull up. As she got out, I looked her over from head to toe, making no effort in disguising my perusal. She was looking good. That long, blonde hair was begging for someone to wrap their hands in it and pull. She had a nice rack and ass, another thing some of my brothers had noticed, much to my irritation. The only thing stopping me from dragging her into the house and having my way with her was the fact that she was Viking's kid.

"So, do you wear that outfit everywhere you go?" I laughed as I checked her out again. The blue, pinstripe dress was short, showing off her long, tan legs. She had to be cold, but I sure appreciated the view.

"I'm heading to work as soon as I'm done here," she said, putting a hand on her hip.

"I'm not criticizing, Kate," I said, smiling slowly, "I'm just imagining what's underneath."

I wasn't usually that blunt when I flirted with her, but I couldn't help myself.

Her face got beet red, but she straightened her spine and walked up to me, hand out. "Keys, please."

Impressed, I dug them out of my right pocket and dropped them in her open palm.

"Thank you," she said, giving me an appraising glance.

When I followed after her, she let out a little huff. She turned around and put a hand on my chest; the pressure was light but firm. "I don't need you here, Mac." She looked up at me. "I'm a big girl, I can handle myself."

I stepped into her so that her palm was flat against my chest. Her fingers curled inward, almost automatically. "I know you can," I told her. "I just like being near you."

She dropped her hand, looking away. The blush never went away when I was around.

To put her at ease, I showed her around, going through the living room then heading to the kitchen. "This whole house needs a shit-ton of work, but whatever you need done, the club will help you out. Whatever needs fixing, just say the word." She just nodded. "You're not much of a talker, are you?"

"Don't have much to say," she mumbled, still not opening up.

"Why is that?"

She shrugged, but I waited, not letting her off the hook. She rolled her eyes, acting put out, but she finally answered. "Just the way I grew up, I guess... It was always best to not say much. It made my life easier."

"I get it, I do…" I gestured for her to follow me as I led her to the back of the house. "I can tell you don't want to talk about it, and that's fine, but you're strong, a survivor."

"Oh?" she asked, sounding surprised by my comment. "You really think so?"

I stopped in the hallway and looked back at her. "Yeah, I do. It took guts to come here, find Viking, and tell him the truth."

Her eyes got wide, and she blinked rapidly a few times. "So...how did you come to be a Desert Sinner?" she asked, not responding to my comment but I could tell my words had affected her.

I waited to answer until we'd reached the bedroom and I leaned against the doorframe. "My parents abandoned me when I was young. They're still alive but I don't speak to them, and it's for the best," I said bluntly. Even though I'd accepted my past, I could admit it still stung, but for the most part, I'd worked through my shit. I'd learned through the club that regrets were a waste of time. Live in the moment, enjoy what you have now, and accept and learn from the past. "If not for the club, and Falcon, his family taking me in as one of their own...I'd probably be dead."

She sighed. "Guess we're both lucky to have found the Desert Sinners, huh?"

"Yeah, we are." Why I was sharing personal shit like this with Kate was beyond me since I'd never really discussed it with anyone. Wolf knew, but that was because we grew up together. I was finding that despite coming from two different worlds, Kate and I had a lot in common. A little uneasy about that realization, I shoved off the doorframe and jammed my hands in the front pockets of my jeans.

"I guess...all the bad stuff happened for a reason," she said, looking at me.

"Makes you appreciate what you have when you finally get it," I said, agreeing with her. "And you'll find that you have it now. I promise, Kate, you won't regret it either. You *are* home. You deserve to have a safe place, and people that'll care and look after you. Even if you're not sure right now, don't forget what I'm saying, okay?"

At that, she gave me a beautiful smile. "You can be nice sometimes, Mac. I didn't know that about you."

I scoffed lightly. "Don't get used to it, *sweetheart*."

At that, instead of a frown, she laughed softly, shaking her head. "I need to get going," she said, moving down the hall. "Thanks for the tour."

When she looked over her shoulder at me, I almost thought she was making sure I was following. I knew, right then, that no matter what, I'd always have her back.

12

KATE

My conversation with Mac occupied my thoughts for most of the day. It was super busy at the diner, so I was pleasantly surprised when I saw Meredith and the boys come in.

The twins rushed me as I was passing off a large, brown tub with dirty dishes to Evelyn across the counter. Meredith gave me a quick hug, like it was something we did all the time. The boys stopped their rambling of what they did at school to plop down at the counter, dropping their book bags on the ground as soon as Pam presented two huge pieces of chocolate pie.

"Sorry to bother you when you're busy!" Meredith said, smiling.

I moved us toward the side near the kitchen door, where there were fewer people. "It's okay, I'm glad to see you," I said. "What brings you and the boys around?"

"Well, every month, I plan a family barbecue. Usually on a

Friday or Saturday since the kids can stay up a bit later. And since you're officially moving into the house this weekend, I figured Saturday night would be as good as any."

She looked at me expectantly, but I had no idea what to say. The idea of being in a room full of bikers tomorrow evening and their idea of a party—

"It's not what you're thinking," Meredith said, cutting right through my thoughts and chuckling. "It's only family, no club girls, much tamer."

I exhaled, not realizing I'd been holding my breath. But those nerves I'd had since I arrived in Vegas ramped up a hundredfold. "The *whole* club will be there?"

She nodded. "Old ladies, kids, close friends of the club. It's fun, very relaxed."

I doubted that, but I had a sinking feeling this was a big deal. She was doing this for me, like some sort of coming out party, or whatever. Viking wanted me to be part of this, part of him. Meredith clearly had no issues, and she was so normal and put together. She knew this world and how to function in it, and maybe she could help me. Actually, I had no doubt she would. I just had to ask.

So, I took another deep breath and made a decision. "Okay," I said. "I'm in."

Meredith's brilliant smile made me smile in return. She gave me another hug that I heartily returned, and by the time she and the twins left, I felt a little more at ease about the barbecue. Then again, I'd be seeing Mac, and god only knew what things he'd say to me to make me blush, but this time, in front of the whole club.

It was seven by the time I got off work, changed at the motel, and then sped all the way to the clubhouse. For the past hour, I was relieved to find that I wasn't put on the spot. I was acknowledged by everyone and welcomed warmly, but no one asked me questions or pried. They let me be and didn't push.

Meredith was always there when I needed her. She eased me through the introductions of the patched members, giving me pointers on conduct, the lingo, and how things worked. Frankly, it was all too much, and I knew I didn't absorb a lot of it, but everyone was patient with me.

The family atmosphere, while unexpected, was wonderful to see. It was hard to fathom this was my life now.

After a couple of hours, I needed some air and found a secluded spot near a few desert willows lining the fence in the backyard. Even though I'd been offered a beer, I'd opted for a ginger ale with lime. I stood there sipping my drink, watching the flames shoot up into the sky from the fire pit. There was just as much activity outside as inside. The grills were still going on the far side of the yard, with people waiting in line for seconds, while a mix of country and rock blared so loud from the speakers I could feel the bass vibrating through my body. Since the clubhouse was situated in an unincorporated area, the stars seemed to blanket the dark sky as far as the eye could see, and it felt like we're on a different planet.

I looped my fingers through the wire fence, seeing nothing but desert and the outline of some rocky mountain I didn't know the name of off in the distance.

Wild and free, that was the motto of the club and out here, they had it. I could see its attraction and its dangers. But mostly, I took into account the things that mattered most to these people: Family. Trust. Honor. Togetherness. Love.

"Hey."

I jumped a little, then relaxed when I saw it was Mac.

"Hey back," I said, heart racing and not just because he'd surprised me.

"Having fun?" he asked, settling next to me and mimicking my stance by looping his fingers through the chain link.

"Yes...no?"

He laughed. "I hear ya," he said. "We party hard, even on family night."

"It's wonderful, actually, everyone getting together. You're all so tight. So close."

"You can be part of it, too, Kate. If you want," he reminded me.

That was both the problem and the solution. "I know..."

"What's stopping you?" he asked, apparently hearing the conflict in my voice.

"Me," I murmured.

"Why's that?"

"Because I don't know what being a part of a family truly

means. The loyalty you hold dear—it's just a vague, unfamiliar concept to me."

"What do you mean?" he asked.

Did I want to tell him my ugly truth? But the words just came out. "My grandmother raised me. She was a wonderful person but she"—I paused, admitting something I'd never once voiced aloud—"didn't love me enough to protect me from her emotionally and verbally abusive husband and son."

In my peripheral view, I noticed it. It was small, but I saw him tense. I could *feel* his anger. For me, on behalf of me. And it was comforting, even though I knew that was probably messed up.

"You know," I said, my voice quiet "when you're told you're nothing and no one tells you that they care about you, that you matter, hug you, or tell you that they love you...it's the slowest way to die, I think."

"Kate...come here," Mac said hoarsely. He pulled me into him, wrapping his arms around me.

I hugged him back, because, dammit, I wanted to know what being in his arms felt like. He held me tight to his body, his hand going into my hair, and I relished the contact.

Mac had a harder edge than most because of his childhood. Even though he found the club early on, that kind of thing haunted a person all the way into adulthood. I knew better than most. He could be honest and open, but already I knew it had to be on his terms. He didn't share with just anybody, and he had a tough time showing his emotions. I could read him easier because our traumas were so similar. Because I was the same exact way. It was nice to know that there was someone here who understood me on a fundamental level. How odd it'd be someone like Mac, but it felt like kismet, or maybe Mom was working her magic.

I pulled away and looked at everything around me; there was a lot to be gained.

When I noticed Mac's hand traveling up and down my back, I realized how...personal our embrace had become. I pulled away further, and he didn't stop me. "You okay?" he asked me, tucking some stray strands of hair behind my ear.

I thought about it. "Better than yesterday," I said.

He grinned. "Glad to hear that."

We headed back to the clubhouse. Even though I was tall, I felt small and delicate next to him.

Just when I was about to tell Mac I appreciated him listening to me, a woman came bolting out of the clubhouse and cuddled right up next to Mac.

"Hey, baby," she started as she rubbed her hand up and down Mac's chest.

"What the fuck are you doing here, Michelle?" Mac growled.

Michelle pouted, her arm like a vice around his waist. "Viper said you guys needed help with bartending. Party's winding down, so I figured we could go up to your room. It's been a while, baby; I miss you."

I felt my stomach bottom out, seeing him with *her*. Meredith had told me about the club girls, and I knew some of the guys hooked up with them. Mac had clearly been hooking up with this Michelle chick. For some stupid reason, I'd thought he was single, but it should have been obvious someone like him would be with somebody. Or a lot of somebodies. Even though he teased me and made a lot of innuendoes, he'd never once made a move on me.

The knot of jealousy in my stomach was embarrassing. So what if he'd been kind to me? It didn't mean anything, especially to Mac, and as much as I hated to admit it, I was more than a little disappointed.

"See you around," I muttered. As I moved around them, I glanced over and met Michelle's eyes. The look of triumph was evident, but I ignored it. I ignored it all and decided to take into consideration all the other good things I had.

While Mac was no knight in shining armor, he'd at least said some wise things I was starting to take to heart. Like deciding that I truly had a place here. As I walked over to Viking and Meredith, who included me like I'd always been there, the sting of disappointment I'd felt with Mac faded.

Slowly, I started to enjoy myself as I listened to a story Colt was telling. And as the night wore on, I found more and more reasons to stay, grateful that my luck was finally turning.

13

MAC

At church the other night, Viking asked if some of us would be willing to help fix up the bungalow for Kate. Even though she'd already moved in, there was painting and a few minor repairs to be done.

I don't know what possessed me to volunteer, but Viking barely asked for help before I was offering to be there. Now, I'd be spending the whole day with Kate. But it might be a different Kate today since she hadn't looked happy the other night when we were interrupted. Frankly, I was getting real tired of Michelle's antics.

Standing by the bar, I checked my phone for the tenth time in the last few minutes. I texted Kate an hour ago that I'd be coming over to help, but hadn't gotten a response. Figures.

As I was getting ready to leave, Michelle, once again, came

from out of nowhere and was all over me. "I haven't seen you since the barbecue," she whined.

"Yup, and there's a reason for that," I said, peeling her off me. "You aren't the only one I hook up with."

She looked like I just slapped her. I didn't know why she acted surprised. She knew what her role was. None of the guys ever promised a club whore more than a quick fuck. If she didn't get that through her head, then she was going to start having a real problem here.

"You're not hooking up with that bitch, are you?" she asked, her face contorting into anger.

I grabbed her by the shoulders and got right in her face. "What the fuck did you just say?"

Fear flashed in her eyes, but then she smirked when she realized my hold on her wasn't enough to hurt. "I was wondering if you've been fucking Viking's daughter."

I looked her right in the eyes and spoke quietly, my fingers digging into her flesh. Her eyes widened at the rage radiating off of me. "First off, you don't get to question me or what I do...*ever*. Are we clear on that?" She nodded her head, so I continued. "And don't ever call Viking's daughter a bitch again. If you do, you won't have to worry about my reaction. Viking will throw you out on your ass so quick, your head will spin."

I pushed her away, making her stumble back. "Fuck you, Mac!" she spat. "You're such an asshole!"

I laughed. She wasn't wrong about that.

"Lady problems?" Wolf asked as he walked in from the kitchen, a beer in his hand.

"That's no lady," I joked.

"When are you heading over to Kate's?" Wolf asked, setting his beer bottle aside and sitting on a stool I'd just vacated.

"In a few minutes."

"She's pretty hot, huh? It's gonna be a good day watching her work."

I didn't like how much interest Wolf showed anytime it had to do with Kate, but I didn't want to encourage him, so I didn't respond.

"On a scale of one to ten, she's like a twenty," Wolf droned on.

Seriously, this asshole was asking for me to punch him in the face. "Dude, you got a death wish? Viking would kill you before he would let you get near his daughter."

"Funny, he must trust me enough because he asked me to watch her and her friend when they go out next week to celebrate her birthday."

"What?" I asked sharply, glancing over at Wolf's smug face. "He asked you to do that?"

"Sure did." He smirked like he knew how much he was getting to me.

That was the bad thing about being friends with someone for as long we had. Sometimes they knew you better than you knew yourself.

"Maybe I can talk him into having you go with me," he added casually, but was watching me too closely.

I shrugged. "Sure, you do that." I slapped his back as I walked away.

"See you over there in a few minutes." He laughed behind me.

I was acting like an idiot with a crush, and Wolf saw right through me. If I wasn't careful, the whole club would catch on.

I rode my bike over to Kate's in case we needed to go pick anything up. When I pulled up to Kate's place, I saw her car, but no one else had shown up yet. As I was getting off my bike, she walked out onto her porch. Even in sweatpants and a zippered hoodie, she was smokin' hot.

"Hi, Mac," she greeted me quietly, once again the shy girl instead of the vibrant one that had started to emerge.

I could tell she was thinking about the other night and Michelle hanging all over me, but, like every time before, I didn't miss how her eyes checked me out. I couldn't remember a time where a female had held my attention like this. I told myself it was because she was off-limits, but that was too easy of an excuse. In truth, she was different, unique...special.

"Hey." I joined her as she walked to her car. "So, what's the plan for today?"

"Painting," she said, popping open the trunk.

We each grabbed a couple of gallons of paint from her car and made our way back inside. Taking a look at the taping she already did, it wouldn't be difficult to finish up before the day ended.

"Where do you want to start?"

I watched her as she bit her bottom lip while she contemplated the best order to do things in. She had an air of innocence about her, and she was oblivious to the fact that she was sexy as sin.

"I think we should start in the bedroom."

"Sounds good to me." I winked at her and loved the blush that started to creep up her cheeks once she realized how I interpreted her suggestion.

"That's not what I meant," she said as she rolled her eyes and shoved my shoulder.

"Oh yeah?" I asked, crowding her space. "Don't think I haven't noticed you checking me out."

"Wh-what?" Yeah, she knew she was caught, but she tried to lie anyway. "I have no idea what you're talking about."

"Sure you don't, sweetheart." I was standing so close to her, I could feel her shiver as my breath fanned over her neck.

Just as I was about to do something stupid, I heard the other guys driving down the driveway. She quickly stepped away from me to meet everyone outside. I followed behind, seeing quite a few of our guys pulling up.

"Oh wow," she whispered as she stood in the doorway.

"What?"

"I didn't expect so many people to come help today."

"You're Viking's daughter; therefore, you're family. That means something around here," I explained.

"Still trying to get used to that." I didn't think she meant for me to hear her, but I did.

"I know," I said. "It's strange at first, but just accept it for what it is, and you won't feel so weird about it, trust me."

We made some quick introductions. Fitz and Hawk had just gotten back from dealing with more of the Phantom shit show and had missed the barbecue Meredith had set up for Kate. Hawk slowly looked her up and down and then turned to me, a stupid grin on his face. It was obvious his asshole brother had been talking shit with him.

We spent the next few hours painting, then fixing up some minor stuff in and around the bungalow. The place was looking good, and I could see that Kate was pretty pleased with it.

"Hey, I'm taking a quick break. Be right back," I told Wolf as I grabbed my pack of smokes from the coffee table. I needed a few minutes to myself. My dick had been in a permanent hard state watching Kate bending over for the last couple of hours. I needed some fresh air before someone caught me eye-fucking our president's daughter.

I had just lit my cigarette when I looked over and saw Kate standing at the other end of the porch, staring at Viking's bike. She hadn't noticed me yet, so I took advantage of that and walked up behind her.

"It's beautiful, isn't it?" I asked, admiring the sleek red beast in front of us.

She jumped a little and spun around to face me. "Oh my god, Mac! You scared me."

"You were staring pretty hard at the bike. Ever been on one?"

She shook her head. "I never knew anyone who rode before."

I was going to ask her to go for a ride with me, but she changed the subject before I had a chance.

"So, thanks for your help today. I can't believe how much we got done."

"The place is looking good." Our hard work had paid off, and it was starting to look like a home.

"Yeah, it is. I think this is going to work out." She sounded surprised.

"So, you've decided you're going to stick around a while?" From my conversation with Viking, it sounded like she still hadn't confirmed what her plans were.

"I think so," she said as she leaned on her forearms against the porch railing, mirroring my position.

I looked over at her and was hit with a sudden and unexplainable need to slam my lips on hers and make her mine. Just then, the front door opened, and her father walked out.

"We're about done in there. Zeke and TJ are putting a few things away, then we're all going to head out," he said to his daughter.

"Thank you so much for everything today." She turned and hugged Viking.

The shocked look on his face made me think this may have been the first time she had done that.

"No problem at all," Viking said, hugging her in return. "If you need anything, give me a call, okay?"

"Will do," she responded with a smile as her dad, and a few other guys, started down her front steps.

"Oh, before I forget, Wolf and Mac are going with you next

weekend when you celebrate your birthday," he announced over his shoulder before he got to his bike.

"What?" she said, confused. "Why?"

He got behind his bike, gunning the engine. "I'm not comfortable with my barely legal daughter hanging out down there without someone watching out for her."

"I don't think that's necessary."

"I do."

She looked like she was about to argue but when she looked at me, I shook my head a little. "Fine. But they better not keep Evelyn and me from having fun," she said in a huff.

Viking just shook his head and laughed.

I couldn't contain my laughter, even as Kate stood there and mumbled something about not needing a babysitter.

I was going to tease her about the many ways *we* could have fun together when I saw her watching the bikes as they drove away.

"Want to go for a ride?" I asked.

I'd never had anyone ride with me before, but this was something I wanted to share with her.

"Really?" She looked both hesitant and excited.

"Yeah. Go inside and put on a pair of jeans and a jacket, then we'll head out."

Suddenly, a huge smile broke out across her face, and she ran into the house like her ass was on fire. A couple of minutes later, she was following behind me as we walked to my bike.

Once there, Kate hesitated for a minute. "What's up?" I asked.

"Uh…" she replied as she stood staring at my bike. "I don't know what to do."

I handed her the spare helmet I kept in my saddlebag. "You don't have to do much. Just hold onto me and don't fight against the movement of the bike," I explained.

When I looked at her, she was biting her lip again. It looked seductive as hell. She took a fortifying breath and got on the bike.

Wanting to take her somewhere I knew she would enjoy, I drove to one of my favorite spots along the Colorado River. It was far enough away from the more touristy areas but still had a beautiful view.

The drive ended much too soon. I was enjoying the feel of Kate's arms around my waist. It had me thinking of other ways I'd prefer to have her wrapped around me.

"Oh wow, this is gorgeous," Kate announced as we walked down to the water's edge.

"Let's go sit down over there." I grabbed hold of her hand and led her over to a large boulder.

I felt her tense slightly at the contact, but she quickly relaxed and didn't pull her hand away. I helped her climb up the rock and sat down next to her. We were quiet for a little bit, enjoying the view.

"So, what else brought you out here, besides looking for your father?" I asked.

"Isn't that enough?" she replied with her own question.

"Normally, I would say yes. But you started telling me a bit about your home life the other night. I had a feeling there was more you weren't telling me."

"Hmm…good-looking *and* intuitive."

"I knew you had been checking me out," I joked, and she rolled her eyes.

"Oh please! You're so cocky."

I just winked at her, and she shook her head. "Anyway, the truth is, I'd been undecided about whether I wanted to meet Viking or not, when my living situation took a turn for the worse."

She stopped talking, but I wanted to know more. "Continue," I prodded.

"You don't want to hear my whole sob story." She tried to make a joke about it, but I could tell it wasn't something small.

"I want to know everything about you," I told her, shocked by my admission. I never cared to learn the small details about the chicks I hooked up with, but I did want to know more about Kate. "It sounded like your childhood was as fucked up as mine. You said your grandmother raised you…?"

"Yes…" She didn't say anything and then, in a rush, "My mom killed herself when I was six years old."

Jesus, that was heavy. When she didn't say anything more, I took her hand and laced my fingers through hers. It seemed to help as she continued her story about how things got worse after her grandmother died.

I didn't understand how people could be so cruel to their own family, but my own parents were proof that just because you were related to someone didn't mean they would love you.

When she started explaining about her friend Jonathan, I interrupted.

"So, this guy… he was just a friend?"

She looked at me, and I realized she heard the hardness in my voice. "Considering you're hot and heavy with that Michelle girl, I don't think you have a right to get mad."

"There's nothing between me and Michelle. Yeah, we used to hook up, but that's over. Been over since I laid eyes on you."

She didn't look convinced but let it drop. "Anyway, after I made it clear we were just friends and would never be anything more, Jonathan and I got into a huge fight, and I drove out here."

"And he was fine with you leaving?" I needed to know more about this Jonathan guy.

"He didn't get a say in it. However, he has texted me a few times since I moved. At first, he tried to apologize, but lately, he's been saying things like we are meant to be together, and he's tired of waiting for me to come to my senses. I've started to ignore his texts."

I didn't like the sound of that. Desperate guys did stupid shit. "You'll tell me if he keeps bothering you?"

"Mac, I appreciate it, but I can handle Jonathan."

"I know you can, but it doesn't mean you don't want or need help, Kate."

She regarded me for a long second before nodding. "You know, I just realized I've been pouring out my heart to you, and I don't even know your real name."

"No one uses my name anymore, but since you shared, I'll tell you. It's Ryan MacIntyre."

"Well, that explains the road name."

Since I wanted to end this day on a better note than last time we were alone together, I stood and pulled her up along with me.

"Where we going now?"

"For a ride in the desert."

Her eyes brightened. "I'd like that."

I took her hand and led her to my bike. At some point, I needed to start thinking about the consequences of making Kate mine. It was inevitable, but I didn't relish the anger Viking would unleash on me.

14

MAC

It had been a long week. Shit with the Phantoms was getting worse. They hadn't made their way to Las Vegas or the immediate surrounding areas, but they were definitely too close for comfort.

Viper and Hawk had a run-in with them at a bar about an hour north of Las Vegas. It had cost the club a pretty penny to keep the two of them out of jail for assault. Hopefully, the ass kicking the two of them handed out sent a message that we weren't going to back down.

We were probably going to be calling in some favors from some of the Desert Sinner charters soon to help deal with them, but that brought its own set of issues. Needless to say, I was looking forward to spending some time with Kate, away from the stress of things out of my control.

I hadn't seen her since the day I took her for a ride. I didn't know what the plan was tonight, but I liked the idea of watching Kate let loose. On the other hand, I wasn't looking forward to hanging out in some club, watching a bunch of lame guys hitting on anything that looked their way. I was going to need to make it clear that Kate wasn't available for the taking.

I knocked on her door and waited for what seemed like forever before Kate answered. When she finally did, I didn't even recognize her. Instead of the usual jeans and sweatshirts she wore, or her ridiculous waitress uniform, she was wearing a skintight, black dress that barely covered her ass. The V in the front went down past her tits, and I couldn't seem to pull my eyes away from her perfect breasts.

"Hello, Mac," she said. Her grin told me she knew exactly what she was doing to me.

"Hey, happy birthday."

"Thank you." Her smile was now sincere instead of teasing, and I liked that one even more.

"Your dad is going to be pissed when he finds out what you're wearing."

"So, you're going to tell on me now? I didn't think big, bad bikers liked snitches," she joked as she pulled on a tight, short leather jacket.

She was trying to rile me up, and it was working. "No, but if he finds out, it's your ass." That wasn't true. If Viking found out what she was wearing, he would kick *my* ass for letting her out of the house dressed like that. "So, what's the plan for tonight?" I asked, looking for anything to get my attention off how sexy she looked and how I wanted nothing more than to bend her over and fuck her right there in the living room.

"I'm going to drive over to Evelyn's house to pick her up. We're definitely drinking and dancing. She even managed to get us some VIP passes, but I don't know where to yet. Who knows what else we'll decide to do." She finished touching up her makeup in the mirror by the front door, and I sat there, mesmerized like a fucking idiot. "You know, this is completely unnecessary. I don't need a babysitter."

"Too bad. Your dad asked Wolf and me to go with you, so that's what's happening." I was a little annoyed she didn't want me to go with her.

"Where is Wolf, anyway?" she asked, just now realizing he wasn't with me.

I tried to tamp down the possessiveness I felt. Wolf had already stated he had no interest in Kate when I questioned him recently. Then he spent the next twenty minutes telling me what an idiot I was for even thinking about hooking up with her. What he didn't understand was there was no longer a question of if I was going to fuck Kate, but rather a matter of when.

"He's going to meet us wherever we end up. He had some shit to handle."

The shit he was handling had to do with our ever-present problem. I couldn't share that with Kate since it was club business, but it was the reason Viking was insistent that Wolf and I go out with her tonight. The Desert Sinners never targeted women or children, but the Phantoms didn't share the same code.

We walked out of her house together toward her driveway.

"Are you going to ride with me?" she asked.

I laughed at that. "No, babe. You'd never catch me in a cage unless I'm dying."

She rolled her eyes at me, and I wanted nothing more than to grab her by her long ponytail and crash my lips on hers. Her sassy attitude was definitely a turn-on.

She walked to her car, and I climbed on my bike that was parked directly behind her. I followed her to her friend's house and waited outside while she went to get her.

When the two of them walked out, it was clear I was going to get in a fight tonight. They both looked hot, and I just knew some douchebags were going to act like fools around them. I followed them as they headed to the Strip. I always hated driving down here. There were too many cars and pedestrians.

Finally, they pulled into one of the casinos and followed the signs to self-parking. "We're going to go check in," Kate announced as she grabbed a small overnight bag I hadn't noticed before from her trunk.

"You're staying here tonight?" Viking hadn't mentioned that to us.

"Yeah, we both wanted to drink and figured it would be better to stay here than try to figure out rides later."

It made sense, but I hadn't made plans to stay overnight. I walked up with her to check in. After she gave the hotel clerk her information, I informed him I needed a room as well, preferably one next to hers.

She looked at me with questioning eyes, but I just shrugged

my shoulders. "Viking said we needed to stay with you all night."

That earned me another eye roll, which just made me chuckle.

"I don't have any connecting rooms left, but we do have two rooms next to each other," the clerk informed us.

I handed over my credit card. "That'll work."

I sent a quick text to Wolf to let him know about the change of plans and asked him to grab a few things for me from the clubhouse.

Wolf: *The two of you staying at the hotel together? Sounds like trouble.*

Me: *Don't I know it.*

15

KATE

"Tonight is going to be so much fun!" Evelyn squealed as soon as we entered our hotel room. "And now that we got a hot bodyguard to watch our every move, things will be even more interesting."

"You can say that again," I muttered to myself as she headed to the bathroom.

Evelyn and I had hit it off on my first day working at the diner, and I instantly knew we were going to be friends. She was as sweet as could be and made every shift we worked together fun. She was a couple of years older than me, but we meshed well. She was one of the few people I'd actually felt close with, even telling her about some of the stuff in my past. I had Viking, and even Mac and Meredith, to thank for that. Before them, I would've never opened up to anyone or felt comfortable letting people see the real me.

One of the things I admired most about Evelyn was not only did she work at the diner to support herself, but she did it while going to nursing school full-time. Her schedule made it difficult for us to spend time together outside of work, which made tonight all the more special. However, I hadn't told her we'd have not one, but two babysitters the whole night. But, from the sound of things, she seemed totally okay with that.

Me? I was both excited and anxious that Mac was here for my birthday, even though Viking had ordered him to be here. I'd even saved some money to buy this dress specifically because I knew he was going out with us. Based on his reaction, he'd liked what he'd seen.

Mac had been busy with club business all week, so I'd hardly seen him. I wanted him to take me on a ride again, but just when things were starting to go somewhere, he was unavailable. Maybe I was reading too much into the moments we had shared recently.

I'd been spending more time at the clubhouse during the day, but I continued to avoid their nighttime activities. I was enjoying getting to know everyone, and I really liked Wolf and Viper; their laid-back vibe made them the easiest to get along with. The club girls were a different story. They seemed to be around all the time, especially Michelle, who gave me dirty looks whenever I was there. I wasn't entirely sure I believed Mac when he said he and Michelle were done. She was the type of girl Mac probably went after, and I was nothing like that. But sometimes, when he was teasing and flirting or being sweet to me, I forgot about that.

Then there was Viking, always calling or texting or stopping by to make sure I was doing okay, and I was starting to get used to someone caring about the smallest things in my life. He was gone for the week, on a "run," and had promised to celebrate my birthday with me and the family when he got back.

"What do we want to do first?" I asked when Evelyn came back into our room. I checked the alarm clock on the table between our queen-sized beds. It was still too early to hit up any clubs, but I didn't want to stay in our room.

"It's your birthday, you decide," she said.

Evelyn had her own unique style. Her black hair was styled in a cute pixie cut, and her makeup was always soft and natural, except for the vibrant red lipstick she wore. I didn't think she realized just how gorgeous she was, but everyone who came into the diner sure noticed. Guys were always asking to sit in her section, and she always made a ton in tips.

"We could walk around downstairs for a little bit," I suggested.

"Sounds good to me. Let's go!" She was full of energy tonight, and I knew we were going to have a great time.

"Let me go next door and tell Mac what we were doing."

"Fine by me. Maybe Mac can escort us instead of just being your bodyguard?" she said, winking at me. "Then again, since I can tell Mac's got his eye on you, I'll just have to find my own guy tonight."

I felt my face heat up. "It's not what you think," I said. "We're...friends."

"Ha! Yeah right," she retorted. "You two were eye-banging

each other in the elevator all the way up to our floor." She gave me a look. "The walls were mirrored, Kate, and I have eyes."

If my face got any hotter, it'd start melting off. "Whatever. So I think he's hot. He's never even tried to make a move on me!"

"You should take it as a compliment," she said, rummaging through her purse. "He's not treating you like a random hookup."

"Maybe," I demurred.

"This is how I see it—he must really like you if he's not rushing you into bed...yet." Her wolfish grin had my insides all tied up at the idea of Mac and me. "It *is* your birthday, bet he'd be more than willing to give you a present: himself, naked-style."

I groaned, the visual of Mac naked now lodged in my brain. Instead of responding, I grabbed her arm and headed to the door. "Let's just go downstairs."

As soon as we stepped out of our room, Mac stepped out of his. His eyes immediately scanned my body, something he seemed to do a lot. "You finally ready to go or did you need more time to talk about me?"

Evelyn burst out laughing.

"Oh my god, you heard all that?" I asked, mortified.

"Well, you're kinda loud," he said, smirking.

Unable to meet his gaze, I followed Evelyn as she walked ahead of us to the elevators.

"Evelyn's right about one thing," he whispered in my ear.

"Oh yeah, what?" I asked, trying to regain my composure, but when I glanced over at him, the look in his eyes had me stumbling, literally.

"I definitely wouldn't mind ending your birthday night together." He steadied me, his hand low on my back. No smirk, no tease, only the truth. "Just say the word, Kate."

With that, he walked ahead of me. I had to clear my head fast before he noticed I was standing in the middle of the hallway with my mouth hanging open in shock at his words.

I forced any wayward thoughts of sex and Mac out of my head, which was difficult to do when he was standing there in front of me as I stepped into the elevator. Once we reached the busy and very loud casino floor, we looked around. It didn't take long before Evelyn and I decided we wanted to try our hand at a little gambling.

Mac laughed at us when he saw us head toward the nickel slot machines. "Don't go spending all your money in one place."

I rolled my eyes at him, yet again. "Don't be mean. I have no idea how to play anything else."

"Not even blackjack?"

"Nope," I said, watching Evelyn take a seat and start to play.

"Well, let me show you."

I glanced back at Evelyn, who gave me two thumbs up and a big smile from her spot at the machine. I shook my head, but followed after Mac, enjoying the view from the back as much as the one from the front.

Mac managed to find a five-dollar table and pulled out a chair for me. After we threw down some cash for chips, I listened to him as he explained the game to me. The table was full, so we were sitting pretty close to each other. I felt his leg brush against mine a few times. I wasn't sure if it was intentional or not, but I leaned a little closer to him, needing to maintain our connection, and he certainly didn't shy away from the contact. When we were this close, it was hard to ignore the strong pull I felt toward him.

His offer to end the night together kept playing like a loop in my head. As much as I wanted to, I didn't believe that he meant it. While my trust in men was slowly on its way to being restored, the idea of rejection—especially from Mac—would be devastating. I could admit that I didn't just have a girlish crush on him. I thought of him as someone who'd be there for me, and maybe something deeper could grow between us. But fear kept me from taking the next step. Hell, I didn't even know if I was ready for him to make a real move on me. My last relationship had been with Jonathan, and while not romantic, it'd been an epic fail. Just thinking about Jonathan made me wince. I'd finally blocked him from my cell, for now, and tried to block him out of my mind on what should be a momentous day for me.

Mac and I played a couple of rounds before Lady Luck struck.

"Oh my god, I got a blackjack," I yelled excitedly when I was dealt a matching Ace and Queen. Then I did something that shocked even me. I leaned over, wrapped my arms around him, and kissed his cheek.

"Sorry," I mumbled, not usually one to initiate physical contact with anyone.

"I'm not," he said, grinning and pulling me closer to him.

But just then, Evelyn came over, declaring she was bored with the nickel machine and begged us to go to the club upstairs.

I pulled away from Mac. Even though I would have liked to have seen what he would've done next, Evelyn was my friend and here to celebrate my birthday. I wasn't going to ignore her in favor of Mac. But before I could take a step to follow after Evelyn, I felt Mac's hands grab my waist.

"Soon, Kate…" he growled, pulling me into his front.

I didn't say anything as he released me. But I couldn't help the slow smile that spread across my face.

Happy birthday to me indeed.

16

MAC

As we headed upstairs, I got a text from Wolf letting me know he was here. He met us out front of the club, where we were moved to the front of the line, thanks to Evelyn's VIP passes. I could see the bouncer debating whether to let us in or not, but one look at the patches on the back of our cuts and he waved us through.

The girls hurried to the bar and ordered a round of drinks. After a few minutes, with their drinks in hand, they moved to the dance floor. Wolf and I stayed at the bar, but my eyes never left Kate. I watched as a couple of guys tried to dance with them. Kate shook her head, and they reluctantly walked away. A couple of songs later, another guy approached her, and I'd finally had enough.

I walked up behind her and wrapped my arm around her waist, pulling her tightly against my chest. The guy who was trying to talk to her quickly turned around after meeting my murderous glare.

"You're driving me crazy," I whispered and then bit down on her earlobe hard enough that she let out a little groan. The sound shot straight down to my dick. I was tired of playing these games with her.

The beat of the next song was a tad bit slower, but instead of pulling away, Kate started to grind her ass into me. It was taking every single ounce of self-control I had not to do something stupid right there in the middle of the dance floor. She raised her arms and started to run her fingers through my hair. In response, I lowered my mouth and began to suck gently on the soft skin of her neck.

I was just about to say something when she spun around in my arms. Leaning up, she whispered in my ear, "Take me up to your room...please."

I didn't give her a chance to say anything else. I grabbed her hand and started leading her to the exit. I stopped and told Wolf to keep an eye on Evelyn, who was still dancing.

He shook his head. "I hope you know what you're doing," he said, grinning at me.

"Not a fucking clue," I admitted as I walked away.

We made our way to the elevators that led up to the hotel rooms. As soon as we were inside, I pulled her to me and finally kissed her. I'd been dying for a taste since the first night I saw her, and I wasn't disappointed. She tasted just as sweet as I expected, with a small hint of the vodka she had been drinking. I thought she was going to be timid, but her tongue was matching mine, stroke for stroke.

I ran my hand up her thigh just under the hem of her short dress. "Didn't like you wearing this out, but I'm definitely a fan now."

I moved my other hand up to grab her long hair. I got a handful and pulled it just hard enough to make her tip her head back, exposing her neck to me. I dipped my head forward and started to nip at her pulse point. The little moans she was making had my dick harder than I could ever remember it being.

When the elevator doors opened on our floor, we moved quickly down the hallway to my room. I pulled the keycard from my pocket and opened the door as fast as possible. She pushed me inside, just as eager as I was.

As soon as the door closed behind us, she pounced on me and quickly pulled off her leather jacket. My hands immediately went to her back so I could work the zipper of her dress down. I knew she hadn't been wearing a bra based on the cut of her dress, but it still didn't stop my surprise at seeing her tits bare. They were a perfect size, maybe just a tad bigger than a handful, and her light pink nipples were begging for my mouth.

As I leaned down to suck on her breasts, her hands went to the zipper on my pants. Her aggressiveness, while a surprise, was turning me on. I shucked off my cut and pulled my T-shirt over my head, and then I started pushing her back toward the bed. When her knees bumped the side of the mattress, she fell back, and I lowered myself on top of her.

I looked at her gorgeous body and decided the black thong

she was wearing had to go. Not taking my time, I simply ripped it off of her. I grabbed her legs and placed her feet up on the edge of the bed. I wanted to be able to really look at her.

Her confidence continued as she spread her legs so I could get an even better look at what she was working with.

"Your mouth wasn't the only thing I've wanted a taste of." I kneeled on the floor between her legs. I leaned forward, inhaling her sweet scent before diving in and licking her pussy.

"Oh my god, Mac, that feels amazing." I continued to lick her, adding a few sucks to her clit until she started writhing on the bed. I held her hips down and proceeded to assault her with my tongue.

I could feel her entire body start to shudder with her impending orgasm.

"Don't stop," she moaned. Finally, she let go, but I didn't stop until her body stopped shaking.

I crawled up her body and kissed her deeply. "I need to get inside you."

"Nobody's stopping you."

I climbed off her and grabbed the condom out of my jeans. Yes, I'd come prepared. I knew eventually I was going to get her in bed.

I opened the foil packet with my teeth and rolled the latex down my hard shaft.

Climbing back onto the bed, I lined myself up with her entrance. "Once we do this, there's no going back. You're mine. Do you understand?"

"Yes, please, I need you."

I pushed into her, needing her too much to be gentle. She felt tighter than anything I had ever experienced before, and it took all my control to not unload right then.

Her loud moan spurred me on, and I started thrusting into her, going as deep as I could. Her nails were digging into my back so hard I was sure she'd drawn blood. I grabbed her right ankle, moving her foot up to rest on my shoulder so I could get a better angle.

"I'm close, babe. I need you to come for me again," I commanded as I teased her clit once more.

Immediately, her body began to shake with her release, and I loved that she responded so well to me.

A couple more thrusts and I was coming as well.

I rolled off of her and took a moment to get my bearings. I knew fucking Kate would be good, but fuck...I couldn't remember a time that had been better than that.

After catching her breath, Kate rolled over and looked at me. Suddenly, she seemed shy. "Can I stay here tonight?"

"You're not going anywhere. I'm not even close to being done with you," I answered before rolling her over on top of me.

I fucked her two more times before we both crashed from pure exhaustion.

Right before I fell asleep, I thought about the fact I was going to have to face Viking eventually. I understood he was protective of her, even more so because he'd missed out on being her father for so long. But he was going to have to deal with us being together because there was no way I was letting her go.

17

KATE

The heat surrounding me was becoming uncomfortable. Mac's heavy arm was draped across my body, and while I didn't want to move out of his embrace, I needed to check in on Evelyn. Mac had asked Wolf to watch out for her, but I was still feeling a little guilty for leaving her behind last night.

Trying to slip out from under the covers quietly, I sat up only to have Mac's arms tighten around me. "Where're you going?"

"I need to go check on Evelyn," I explained, managing to finally break free of his hold and stand up.

"Evelyn's fine. Wolf was watching her."

"That's what I'm worried about," I joked. I had seen Wolf at the clubhouse, and he almost always had some random girl hanging all over him.

"Why?" he asked.

"It's just, Evelyn's a sweet girl."

"Oh, and you're worried the big bad Wolf had his way with her?" he chuckled.

"Maybe."

I looked around for something to put on, but only saw my dress since all my clothes were still in my room next door. I turned to Mac and saw him sliding on his jeans. He was going commando, and I had no idea why that was hot, but...god, it was.

He caught me staring and flashed me a sexy grin. "You look like you're ready to go another round."

As tempting as that was, I really did need to get dressed and check on Evelyn.

"Actually, I was going to ask you to go next door and get my clothes." I tried to sound like his shirtless body had no effect on me, but I was sure I failed.

"Sure thing, babe." He winked at me.

Just as he reached for the handle, we heard a knock. I quickly covered up with the sheet, but stayed where I could see who it was. As Mac pulled the door open, I was surprised to see Wolf on the other side.

"Have a good night?" he asked as he walked right past Mac and into the room.

He took in the scene in front of him—a half-dressed Mac and me, obviously naked under the sheet.

"Fuck off," Mac responded as he moved to block Wolf's view of me.

"Just wanted to come over and let you know Evelyn is fine. She's still sleeping, and I didn't fuck her." He looked at me when he said that.

Suddenly, I was embarrassed. If he heard that, I could only imagine what else he must have heard through the thin walls last night "Umm…"

I could hear both Mac and Wolf laughing at my embarrassment.

"I also thought you might want your things," Wolf said, as he tried to step closer to hand me my bag.

"Thank you. And I didn't mean anything bad about you maybe hooking up with Evelyn. I know how irresistible you guys can be. I'm trying to watch out for my friend."

"No worries, Kate. It's all good."

"Dude, move away from my girl," Mac growled.

Wolf just shook his head, laughing. "See you guys later."

"Was that necessary?" I asked as soon as the door closed behind Wolf.

"Yes. He doesn't need to be looking at what's mine since he's apparently irresistible."

I rolled my eyes. "Someone sounds jealous."

Teasing apparently riled him up because before I knew it, I was being pressed down against the mattress, my hands held tightly above my head. "You bet your fine little ass I'm jealous. Last night, I told you exactly what was going to happen." He bent down and bit on my neck roughly. "What did you agree to last night?"

I could barely think, he was driving me crazy. I wrapped my legs around him, trying to pull him closer to where I needed him.

"Answer me," he growled.

"That...uh..." He pulled back, waiting for me to tell him what he wanted to hear. "I'm yours."

With a glint in his eye, he suddenly flung the sheets off the bed and proceeded to fuck me harder than I'd ever been before.

Two hours later, it was close to checkout time, so we had to get ready to leave. I was sad our time together was coming to an end. We started to get dressed for the second time this morning when Mac caught me off guard.

"I'm going to talk to Viking as soon as he comes back into town."

"What?" I wasn't expecting that.

There was no way I was ready to tell my father about me and Mac. Our relationship, or whatever it was, just started. More importantly, I didn't want Viking to think any less of me. Like I was a dumb girl hooking up with just anybody.

Mac must have heard the nervousness in my voice because he asked, "What's the problem?"

"I just think this"—I motioned between the two of us—"it just happened last night. Do we really need to tell him anything yet?"

I could see a hint of anger in his eyes. "Let's get something straight right the fuck now. You're either mine, or you're not. You're either in this, or it's not happening. I'm not going to play games with you. We've been doing that for weeks, and I'm done. Decide now what you want." He stood there with his arms crossed in front of his chest, staring at me, waiting for me to get my shit together.

"I'm in. I want to be with you." It was the truth. "But, I don't want to cause any issues between you and my dad, Mac. You know he's going to be pissed about this, right?"

His jaw tightened, but I knew I'd made my point. "I'm not hiding shit," he said, brokering no further argument.

I understood where he was coming from. The Desert Sinners were a true brotherhood, where trust and respect were the two most important things they gave to each other. I couldn't fault him for treating this situation the same as he would anything else that concerned Viking.

I'd figured out early on that Mac was his own man and while he respected Viking greatly, he still had his own opinion and did things his way. I didn't doubt his sincerity about wanting to be with me, especially if he was willing to risk Viking's anger. It felt like I was officially part of this new world I'd entered, and it was both terrifying and exhilarating.

"And when it comes to Viking, I'm going to be honest with him," Mac continued. "He deserves more than my disrespect by hiding what's going on with his daughter."

"I get it. I'm just nervous."

"I understand, but it's going to happen. You have a few days to decide if you want to be there with me or not when I talk to him. But I am talking to him the minute he returns."

"I'll be there," I said, with no hesitation, and judging by the smile on his face, I knew I'd made the right decision.

18

MAC

I wanted Kate to ride with me back home, so we stopped by Evelyn's room to ask if she could take Kate's luggage and drive her car home. She would stop by later to pick it up. Evelyn had no problem with that and Wolf promised to follow her home to make sure she made it okay.

We walked to where I'd parked in the garage, and I shoved a couple of things into my saddlebag. When I turned to face Kate, she was looking up at me from under her incredibly long eyelashes, smiling.

"What's that look for?"

"Just thinking about wrapping my arms around you while we ride," she answered.

I leaned forward and gave her a quick but passionate kiss. Now that we had spent the night together, I couldn't get enough of her.

We got on the bike, and I decided not to head home right away. I wanted to be able to spend time with her alone, without raising suspicions.

A few days later, while I was working at the shop, Kate walked in. I knew she wasn't here to see me since we were keeping things quiet until Viking came back, but that didn't stop me from wanting to pull her to me and have my way with her. I tamped down those thoughts and walked over to her.

"Hey there." She glanced at me from under her long eyelashes, looking sexy as fuck.

She was so tempting, I almost didn't care if someone caught us, but I knew that would be bad for all of us. "Hey, what are you doing here?" I asked instead.

"I came to see Meredith. Is she around?"

Not only had Kate been developing a relationship with Viking, but it appeared she and Meredith were getting closer as well. Even with Viking out of town, she was spending time with Meredith and her brothers, and making an effort to get to know everyone in the club. She didn't realize it, but it reflected well on her that she wanted to be one of us. She still had a lot to learn and understand the rules, but I liked that she wasn't afraid to voice her opinions or ask questions.

"Hi, sweetie. Thank you so much for coming by today," Meredith called from her office door.

"No problem at all," Kate replied, walking over to the office.

Just as she was about to enter, she turned around a gave me a quick wink over her shoulder. I usually enjoyed her playfulness, but right now, she was testing my self-control.

A while later, she emerged and gave Meredith a quick hug goodbye. She then stopped by my station before heading out.

"Everything good?" I asked.

"Yeah, everything's good. Meredith's having a girls' night out next weekend with some of the other old ladies," she explained. "And since I want to spend more time with Finn and Gunnar, they're going to spend the night at my place, so she doesn't have to rush home."

"That's cool. You guys will have a blast."

"I hope so," she said, fidgeting. "I don't have a clue what thirteen-year-old boys want to do on a Saturday night."

"All you need to do is grab a couple of pizzas, rent an action movie, and they'll be fine."

"That sounds like a solid plan." She took a look around the shop before adding, "I really want to kiss you right now."

"Babe, you're killing me. I'll stop by later tonight. Sound good?"

She nodded her head and smiled. "I can't wait."

19

KATE

The last few days with Mac had been incredible. The night I met him, I thought he was the most gorgeous man I'd ever seen. But I was quickly learning there was so much more to him than good looks. The two of us had connected on a level I hadn't expected. I felt comfortable talking about my childhood in greater detail, and he'd even started to help me sort out my feelings on my mom's suicide, something I'd never really come to terms with. While Mac had resolved his issues with his parents abandoning him, he shared a lot on how he dealt with it growing up, and the fact that they were still alive and still wanted nothing to do with him. He didn't hide his emotions with me like he did with everyone else.

I couldn't get enough of him, and it was the same for him. He, of course, had club things to deal with and I had to work, but all of our free time was spent together. However, sneaking around was taking a toll on both of us.

Mac had to be careful when sneaking over to my place, often leaving the clubhouse late at night and walking back before the sun rose. But it was the only time we could be alone together.

I'd just walked in the door from my lunch shift and saw Mac sitting on my couch.

"Hi," I greeted him as he got up and stalked over to me.

His lips came crashing down on mine. Automatically, my hands went to his hair where I pulled gently on the longer strands. My god, Mac could kiss. I could be content just kissing him. Well, that wasn't true. I was lucky to know just how good he was at other things, and I didn't want to miss out on those either.

"I missed you today."

I didn't want to sound too needy, but I could tell Mac liked hearing how much I wanted and needed him.

"What's the plan tonight?" I asked, hoping the two of us could have a relaxing evening eating dinner and maybe watch a movie. Viking was still out of town, so we were keeping a low profile. We didn't want anyone going to him before we had a chance to sit down and talk to him.

"I'm hanging out here until I have to head over to the club-house for church, then I'll be back."

"Church? Is Viking back? I wasn't expecting him until tomorrow." I tried not to sound too frantic, but I was sure I failed.

As much as I enjoyed building a relationship with my father,

I was nervous about sitting down with him and explaining that I was dating Mac. What if he didn't approve? Our relationship was still so new, I had no idea how Viking would react.

"I think Colt's running the meeting tonight and Viking's calling in from the road. Sometimes when he's on a run, he has things to share that can't wait until he gets back."

Mac continued to kiss my neck as my hands played with the button of his jeans. "I guess we should be quick then, shouldn't we?" I said with a grin as I gently pushed him back down on the couch.

I didn't know what it was about Mac, but I'd become insatiable around him. Actually, I knew exactly what it was. I'd never been with anyone that made me feel beautiful and wanted before.

I sunk down to my knees in between his legs, making quick work of the button on his jeans. He was already hard, which wasn't uncommon when we were together. His desire for me made me feel sexy and confident.

I yanked down his jeans and boxer briefs, freeing his massive cock. I had been with a couple of guys before Mac and no one compared to him. I took him in my hand, giving him a few strokes before taking him in my mouth.

The minute my tongue touched his tip, a low moan escaped his lips, and he closed his eyes. Feeling bold, I took him in as far as I could. His hands came up to gently cup my head. He didn't force me down further, but instead guided me to the perfect rhythm. We were both lost in the pleasure I was giving him when he quickly pulled me off.

"I've got to get inside you," he said as he pulled my dress up over my head. He wasn't going to get any argument from me.

He reached down to his jeans on the floor and pulled a condom out. While he covered himself and pulled off the rest of his clothing, I finished removing my bra and panties.

"Up," he directed as he playfully smacked my ass. "I've imagined you bent over this couch for a while."

I needed him just as much as he needed me, so I hurried over to where he wanted me. The second I leaned over, he slammed into me from behind. He felt amazing. I couldn't get enough.

He reached around me, gently rubbing the one spot that was sure to make me see stars. He kept up his intense pace until he felt me shatter beneath him. It only took a few more strokes before he was following me over the edge.

I felt wrung out and could barely move. Mac laid down on the couch and pulled me on top of him. We were both naked, and it was cold in my house, but I didn't want to move. Instead, he pulled down the blanket I kept on the back of my couch and covered us.

"That was amazing," I whispered. I was totally content at that moment and could have stayed there forever.

Unfortunately, the moment didn't last long. "Get the fuck away from my daughter!" a booming voice yelled from my entryway, nearly causing me to fall off the couch.

Why was Viking in my house? He wasn't supposed to be home yet. I couldn't believe this was happening and couldn't hide my complete mortification. I was suddenly very grateful for the blanket Mac had pulled down over the two of us. I sunk further into the couch, my cheeks feeling like they were on fire. I closed my eyes, hoping this was just some crazy nightmare, and if I kept them closed, everything would go away in just a minute.

Unlike me, Mac appeared to be perfectly calm. He slid out from under me, grabbing his jeans and putting them on before speaking in a steady voice.

"Viking…" he started, but was quickly interrupted.

"You!" He pointed at Mac. "Church. Now!" Then he turned his focus on me. "You and I will talk about this later."

Viking had never talked to me like that before, and I was pissed. But before I could say anything, Viking had already turned around to leave, the front door slamming behind him.

"Mac?" I needed reassurance from him that everything was going to be okay.

Instead, he said, "I've got to go," as he put his shirt and cut back on.

"So, Viking says jump, and you just do what he says? You didn't say anything while he yelled at us!" Not only had my father just treated me like I was a teenager getting caught in her parents' house, but Mac hadn't defended us at all.

"Don't do that! He's my president. If he tells me to get my ass to church, I do it. But don't think for one minute I won't fight for you." He raked his hand through his hair. "You have to look at it from his side. He just walked in and found his daughter, one he just started a relationship with, naked with one of his brothers. He knows my history. If I were him, I would have reacted the same way, probably worse."

I continued to sit on my couch, the blanket wrapped around

me tightly. Mac was right, but I was still upset. This wasn't the way I wanted Viking to find out about us.

Mac walked over and kissed me on the top of my head. "I'll be back as soon as I'm done. Don't worry, baby. Everything will be fine."

I wanted to believe him, but what if it was all about to end, just when things were starting to get good. However, one of the things I'd been learning about the club was rubbing off on me: I had to fight for what I wanted. And I was going to fight for Mac, and I'd do whatever it took to make it right with my father.

20

MAC

As I walked toward the clubhouse from Kate's bungalow, a thought occurred to me. Viking barged into Kate's house, like he knew what he was going to see in there. He hadn't acted surprised, just angry. That meant someone had given him a heads-up. I couldn't imagine any of my brothers throwing me under the bus. Besides, the only one who knew anything was Wolf.

Speaking of the devil, I spotted him standing by the fire pit, drinking a beer. I stomped over to him, ready to throw down with my best friend if he'd gone behind my back.

"Did you say something to Viking?" I stood just a few inches away, staring him directly in the eyes.

He looked me up and down and must have noticed my clenched fists. "Dude, you better back the fuck up. I have no idea what the hell you're talking about."

"Mac, Wolf, church now!" Colt yelled from the back door.

We both turned to walk into the clubhouse. I could tell from Wolf's reaction that he hadn't said anything. Speaking in a quiet voice, I quickly explained what happened back at Kate's place.

"Someone must have told him. Viking came storming into her house, knowing full well what he was going to find."

"Who else knows about the two of you?" Wolf asked, keeping his voice low.

"I didn't think anyone did, other than you."

"You need to deal with Viking first, and then we'll figure out who's been talking about shit they shouldn't be."

Wolf walked into the room first. When I entered, I was immediately greeted with a fist to my left cheek. I stumbled a few feet to the right before catching myself. For an older guy, Viking still had a nasty right hook. That hurt like a bitch.

I knew I had it coming, so I didn't retaliate. Instead, I walked over to my usual seat at the table, rubbing my jaw, and waited for the meeting to get started. While the brothers looked at me with raised eyebrows, they knew better than to ask any questions. Viking wouldn't punch an officer of the club without a damn good reason.

"Okay, let's call this meeting to order. We found out the Phantoms are continuing to look for an easy route from Phoenix up into Canada. What we haven't figured out is why they think Vegas is their best option, especially since that means going to war with us. They have to be getting assistance from somewhere, but we haven't figured out who's helping them yet. We need to stay alert, boys." Viking looked directly at me before continuing.

"Can't have any distractions. We also need to call in some rein-forcements."

"The Reno charter would probably be our best bet," Colt suggested. "Their president, Ice, is known to be a dick, but since they're on the route north of here, they probably wouldn't be too happy about the Phantoms going through their town either."

"Agreed," Viking stated. "Let's set up a meeting with them soon. Next item of business, we have a large delivery to make in Los Angeles next week. Colt, Viper, and Mac—you'll be riding with me on this one."

Being chosen for a run to L.A. wasn't unusual, but I couldn't help but wonder if Viking was sending me on this one to keep me away from his daughter.

"When do we head out?" I was glad Viper asked the question. I figured it was in my best interest to keep quiet until Viking and I had time to talk privately.

"We're leaving on Wednesday. Miller's hosting a big party on Friday, and he wants his party favors before then."

Miller was a huge Hollywood producer who split his time between Los Angeles and Las Vegas. We'd provided some coke for one of his parties here a few years ago, and he'd been a loyal client ever since. It didn't hurt that we were known for the purity and high quality of our product. This, along with the security we provided during our drops, resulted in an extremely lucrative business.

"Got it," Viper responded.

"That's it for now. Meeting's adjourned. Mac, stay." Viking slammed his gavel on the solid oak table.

Wolf slapped my back as he passed by while I watched everyone file out. Viking remained seated. After the last guy closed the door behind himself, the two of us sat in silence. I was going to wait for Viking to start the conversation. If I jumped in first, I would sound defensive and made it appear as though I'd done something wrong.

"Mind telling me what I walked in on back at Kate's place?"

"I think it's pretty obvious what that was." Even though it was incredibly stupid, I couldn't hold back my chuckle.

"Now's not the time to be a smartass, Mac." Viking's voice was calm, but I could see the anger in his eyes. "Kate's not another piece of ass for you to use whenever you feel the urge to fuck."

"I'm going to stop you right there." Viking may have been my president, but I wasn't going to let him talk shit about what Kate and I were doing. "I haven't treated her like a piece of ass. We were planning on telling you, together, as soon as you came back to town. We thought you'd be home tomorrow. We sure as hell didn't want you seeing us together like that."

"How long has this been going on?"

"Honestly, I wanted her the night she came here looking for you, but nothing happened until her birthday."

"So, I tell you to protect my daughter, get her comfortable with the club, and you take that as an open invitation to sleep with her?"

I leveled him a look. "It wasn't like that."

Viking regarded me for a second, and I could tell he knew it wasn't. "How serious are you two?" he asked, eyes narrowing.

"Serious enough that I would claim her as my old lady right now if I didn't think it would freak her the hell out."

I saw the small smirk on Viking's face. "I think I need to have a chat with her. Are you heading back over there?"

"I was planning on it, but I'll hang here and give the two of you some privacy."

The two of us got up and walked out to the main room together. Just as Viking reached the door, I remembered I still had a question for him.

"Hey, earlier you came storming into her house like you knew what we were up to."

He nodded his head. "I was told Kate had been looking for me and needed to see me right away. Obviously, that wasn't true. When I got to her house, I saw you guys through her front window. Don't worry, I'll be dealing with the person who set you up."

"Anything I need to be worried about?"

"Nah, just a questionable hookup coming back to haunt you."

Now, I had a pretty good idea who set me up. And I also understood why Viking was concerned about me being with his daughter.

I headed over to the bar, signaling for TJ to bring me a beer while I waited for Viking to finish talking to Kate.

There was a hockey game on, and now that Las Vegas had a team, we finally had someone to root for. Halfway through the second period, I heard the annoying clack of stripper heels behind me. Before I knew it, a pair of arms wrapped around me from behind. The smell of some cheap-ass perfume invaded my senses. Unfortunately, I recognized it and briefly wondered how I'd ever tolerated it.

"Hey, sweetie."

"I suggest you get your damn hands off me." I didn't turn around to look at her. I wanted nothing to do with Michelle.

"C'mon, Mac." She started to pout. "I know you miss me. No one sucks your dick like I do." She whispered that last part in my ear, but judging by TJ's goofy ass grin, he'd heard it too.

I let out a huge guttural laugh. "You've got to be fucking kidding me. First of all, you're delusional if you think I've missed you. And second, I've had way better blowjobs than the ones you give, so don't flatter yourself."

"I would think if Kate was keeping you satisfied, you wouldn't be so grumpy."

With my suspicion now confirmed, I stood up and got in her face. To her credit, she didn't back down.

"I need you to listen very carefully because you clearly didn't get it the first time. From here on out, you don't talk to me. If you see me around, find somewhere else to be. And you most definitely don't talk to or about Kate. I don't think pissing off Viking is in your best interest."

I didn't wait for a response; instead, I headed outside. I wouldn't go to Kate's house until I knew she and Viking were done, but I didn't want to hang out in the clubhouse any longer. I walked over to the fire pit and took a seat on one of the wooden chairs.

I heard someone walking up behind me. "Hey, man. You good?"

I glanced over at Wolf as he sat down on the chair next to mine.

"Stupid drama with a bitch inside. But other than that, yeah man, I'm good. I'm actually better than good."

Wolf laughed. "You're serious about Kate, aren't you?"

It wasn't really a question, and I was tired of explaining myself to people, so I stayed silent.

"Man, I never thought I'd see the day when your ass decided to settle down with a chick. On top of it, you picked the President's daughter." Wolf shook his head. "But I shouldn't be surprised. When you decide to do something, you usually go big."

He had a point. No one would accuse me of ever taking the easy road in life.

We talked a little bit about some club shit, but I quickly became antsy. I took a drink of my beer. "I wish Viking would hurry up. I need to go make sure she's okay."

Wolf just shook his head. "Yeah, you've got it bad."

21

KATE

I heard a knock on my door, but I didn't feel like answering it. The only person I wanted to see was Mac, and he'd walk in, not knock.

"Kate, can you please open the door? I want to apologize."

Well, that was unexpected. I doubted Viking made a habit of apologizing to anyone. Since it would be rude of me to leave him hanging out there, I walked to the door and opened it.

"Hi, can I come in?" he asked, and I could hear the remorse in his voice.

I shrugged my shoulders. "It's your house," I said coolly, still pretty pissed off.

He laughed as he walked past me on his way inside. It looked like he was headed toward the couch but at the last minute he detoured over to the recliner. A small laugh escaped when I realized why he was avoiding the sofa.

"Do you want something to drink?"

"A beer would be great."

I walked to my kitchen and grabbed a bottle out of the fridge. I handed him his beer and then took a seat on the couch. Since it'd been my naked ass on it, I had no problem sitting there.

Viking took a couple of sips and then looked at me. "Kate, I'm sorry for barging in here earlier tonight. I had no right to do that. You're an adult and deserve privacy. I should have respected that."

I was so caught off guard, I was unable to respond. Instead, I just sat there and stared at him, so he continued.

"This is all new to me. I wasn't there to protect you when you were growing up, and I feel like I'm trying to make up for it now. I'm going to fuck up. But it will never be my intention to hurt you."

The emotion welling up inside of me was threatening to break free, and I knew I wasn't going to be able to hold back the tears.

Sure, I may have been mad at Viking, but I knew he was coming from a good place. This man had accepted me into his life, no questions asked. His actions were his way of showing me how much he cared. It was something I hadn't realized I was missing, but now that I had the love of a father, I didn't ever want to lose it.

The tears started to fall down my cheeks.

"Shit! Kate, I'm sorry. Please don't cry."

That had me laughing. I'm sure I looked like a crazy person, laughing hysterically while crying.

"I'm not crying because I'm upset. I went all my life not having a dad around to care for me." He looked like he wanted to interrupt, so I put my hand up and continued. "You know I don't blame you for that. But it doesn't change the fact that I never experienced love like that when I was younger. And even though I came into your life unexpectedly, you've taken on that role. It just feels good to know you care about me and it's not just for show. You mean what you say and follow it up with actions. Thank you."

A couple of months ago, I would've been too scared to pour my heart out like that. The possibility of rejection would've kept me from being honest about my feelings. But Viking had proven himself to me. I saw how he treated his wife, his sons, and his brothers in the club. All of them were his family, and he made it clear I was a part of that family. I knew he wouldn't turn his back on me. At first, I'd been concerned about the fact that they're an outlaw club, but it didn't worry me anymore. There was more good than bad, and I knew I was willing to accept both.

"You don't have to thank me for loving you. I know it takes a lot for you to trust, but you don't ever have to doubt my love for you."

I couldn't contain myself any longer. I jumped up from the couch and launched myself at my father. I hugged him so tightly I wasn't sure he could still breathe. "I love you too, Dad."

When I finally pulled away, I could see the glisten in my father's eyes. This was a moment I would never forget. It's when I honestly felt like I belonged in this family. I doubted my father would forget it either.

After a few minutes, he got up to go home.

"One more thing. Mac is going to head over here after I leave. Don't worry about his face. I didn't hit him… that hard."

"Dad! You hit him?"

"Darlin', he knew he had it coming," he said firmly. "I may be okay with you and him being together, but no dad wants to see what I did earlier."

I could feel my face heating up. "Got it," I mumbled, also hoping he never saw me and Mac having sex ever again.

I followed him out and hugged him around the middle before he left. His soft smile and look had me almost tearing up again. It was a nice feeling that I had both guys in my life. A life that was just beginning, and far better than I could have dreamed.

22

MAC

"She's all yours, don't fuck it up." I heard Viking before I saw him come out of the clearing from Kate's place.

"I don't plan on fucking it up." That was the truth. Now that she was mine and everyone knew, I had no plans on letting her go.

I tossed my beer bottle in the trash and told Wolf and Viking I would see them both tomorrow.

As I walked to Kate's, I realized I needed her to understand this was it for me. We were together, and that meant something to me.

When I climbed up her porch, I could see her sitting on the couch through the living room window, the soft light of the lamp casting her in a beautiful glow. She looked like an angel, completely serene.

I walked in the door quietly, not wanting to disrupt her

moment. When she heard the soft click of the door behind me, she looked up. The beautiful smile on her face nearly knocked me off my feet.

The moment I first saw her, I thought she was the most stunning woman I'd seen, but this smile, it made her beauty shine bright.

Then I looked at her eyes, and they were red-rimmed. I instantly went on alert. What the hell had Viking said to her?

"Baby, what's wrong?" I kneeled in front of her.

"What?" She shook her head. "Nothing's wrong."

She looked at me and gasped. "He said he didn't hit you that hard!"

"What? Oh, this?" I pointed at my cheek and grinned. "Don't worry about it, it's all good. Now you wanna to tell me why you're crying?"

She laughed and then wiped her face with the sleeve of her sweatshirt. "These are happy tears," she said.

"Babe, care to explain?"

She proceeded to tell me about her conversation with Viking. She had finally come to terms with the fact that the man was completely genuine when it came to his long-lost daughter.

And for the first time, I felt confident that she was going to stay here. I'd been completely serious when I told her she was mine, but I wasn't convinced I wouldn't eventually be chasing her down somewhere. But now she finally seemed to believe she belonged here.

"That's some good stuff, baby." I leaned in and kissed her. As usual, there was nothing sweet or gentle about our kiss. But, before we got too hot and heavy, I needed to break the bad news to her.

I pulled back from our kiss, and she looked at me, her brows furrowed. "Even though I hate to mess up all the good shit going on right now, I need to tell you that a few of us are heading out soon. I'm not sure how long we'll be gone. Hopefully, it won't be more than a few days."

"Oh." I could see the happiness drain right out of her.

I hadn't gone out of town since right after she moved to Las Vegas, and while a part of me was itching for a good long run with the guys, I didn't want to leave her.

"Where are you going?"

"That's club business." She rolled her eyes at my explanation but didn't say anything. Considering how things were going, the fewer people who knew what we were up to, the better.

"When do you leave?"

"On Wednesday."

"That's in two days!"

"Hey." I lifted her chin with my finger. "The sooner I leave, the sooner I'll be back here with you."

She laughed. "Wow, Mac, that almost sounded romantic."

"Yeah, well, don't get used to it. I'm not a romantic guy, but I'm ready to get in that pussy." I smiled as I pulled her up off the couch.

"There's the Mac I know," she said as she followed me to her bedroom.

Once in there, I lifted her up and tossed her on the bed, where

I proceeded to show her just how much I would miss her while I was gone.

A loud chime woke me up. Kate and I must have passed out after our intense round of sex. I looked over to the nightstand where her phone was sitting. It went off again, and when it lit up, I saw a text from an unknown number. The preview had enough for me to figure out it was from that asshole, Jonathan.

Clearly, I needed to make another stop while I was in L.A. When I had found out our destination for our run, I decided I was going to stop at her uncle's house. I planned on getting a few things she'd mentioned she hadn't been able to get, like a box of photos, and having a word with her dipshit uncle.

Now, I needed to have a word with Jonathan as well.

Kate rolled over and snuggled into my chest. Making plans for handling the two assholes that had hurt my girl could wait. For now, I wanted to enjoy having her in my arms where she was safe. Tomorrow, I would tell Viking about my plans. I didn't think he would have a problem with the extra stops. If I knew him at all, he would be standing right there beside me making sure our message was clear: No one would hurt Kate again.

23

KATE

The guys had left two days ago, and I was already missing Mac like crazy. It seemed impossible that I could have developed such strong feelings for him in such a short amount of time, but I knew what I was feeling was the real deal. And now that I had my dad's approval, everything felt right.

"Happy looks good on you."

I spun around and saw Evelyn standing in the doorway of the diner's kitchen.

"What are you talking about?" I asked, but couldn't wipe the smile off my face.

"Oh, stop it. You've had the same look every day since we went out for your birthday. It wouldn't have anything to do with a certain biker, would it?"

I couldn't help it; I blurted out everything that had happened since that night. It was nice having a friend I could share things with.

"Oh, hun, I'm so happy for you. I could tell by the way Mac looked at you that he was crazy about you."

"I'm crazy about him too," I admitted.

"Well, why are you still here? Go see your man."

"Actually, he's out of town. I'm going to hang out with my brothers tonight instead," I said as I took off my apron.

"That's awesome. Sounds like things are working out for you here in Vegas."

They really were, and I couldn't have been happier.

I said goodbye to Evelyn and Pam and made my way to my car. As I opened my door, I heard my text alert go off. Hoping it was Mac, I quickly grabbed my phone and checked my messages.

My excitement turned to annoyance when I saw it was another text from Jonathan.

Jonathan: *I need to see you. Stop ignoring me.*

I'd blocked his number, but he must have gotten another one. I was going to have to block him again, but first I wanted to make it clear we had nothing to talk about. The more time I spent with the club, the more I saw the difference between a relationship where the person truly cared for you and what I had with Jonathan.

Me: *There isn't anything to discuss anymore. You need to stop contacting me.*

Jonathan: *This isn't over! You can't get rid of me that easily.*

A shiver ran down my spine at his words. Why couldn't he leave me alone? He was starting to scare me. Maybe it was time for me to change my number.

That was something I could figure out later. For now, I blocked his new number on my phone and hoped he would go away.

I checked the time and saw that it was hitting six already. I needed to get over to Meredith's to pick up Finn and Gunnar. I was excited to get a whole night with my brothers. Sure, they could be super annoying, just like any other teenagers, but I loved spending time with them. After twenty years as an only child, I welcomed every moment of hanging out with my brothers.

"Thank you so much for taking them tonight," Meredith said as the four of us walked out of her house. "I hope you guys have a great time."

"I'm sure we will. You enjoy your night out. You deserve it."

I knew the time Viking spent out on the road was hard on her and the boys. In addition to that, she was responsible for keeping the shop running, taking care of her sons, and dealing with various events for the families of the club. She needed a chance to unwind.

We started to drive toward my house, the boys arguing about

which movie we would watch first. I was wrapped up in the playful banter, I hadn't noticed the truck behind me that was following entirely too close. We weren't too far from my place, so I didn't think too much about it until I felt the hard hit on the back driver's side.

I could feel my car hit the gravel on the side of the road, and I tried to straighten back out, but I must have overcorrected because I started spinning. Before I knew it, we were headed straight toward a ditch. My car went headfirst into it, and I must have hit my head on impact because suddenly everything went black.

24

MAC

The drop we had traveled to L.A. for had gone as well as expected. We made arrangements with Miller for another party he was hosting in Vegas. We'd only been gone for two days, but I was itching to get back home. I'd never been desperate to get back to a chick before, and surprisingly, it didn't bother me. Things were easy with Kate. We wanted to be together, so we were. There wasn't any drama attached to it. It didn't hurt that she had come to accept the club life.

As eager as I was to get home, we had two more stops to make. We needed to exact a little revenge on Kate's jerk of an uncle, and a warning needed to be issued to the cocksucker who wouldn't accept that Kate was never going to be his. I figured both stops would be quick; it was unlikely either of them would give us much trouble.

We pulled up to the first house, and Viking stated he was

going to handle this one. He had a history with Stuart and had a few things he needed to get off his chest.

We walked up the door and Viking proceeded to knock harder than necessary, he barely had control of his fury.

It was early afternoon, but according to Kate, her uncle didn't work. There was a car in the driveway, so we were sure he was home. We could hear some movement before the door swung open.

"What the fuck?" was the only thing Stu managed to say before Viking's fist went flying, crashing into the asshole's jaw.

Stu hit the doorframe hard and then fell to his ass in the entryway. A couple of guys came flying out of the kitchen, the shouting more than likely gaining their interests.

"I suggest you two stay out of this," I warned as Viking dragged Stu up off the ground by the collar of his shirt.

"Why the fuck are you here?" Stu questioned while trying to spit the blood out of his mouth.

Viking pushed Stu up against the wall, his forearm against the struggling man's throat.

"I'm Kate's father, you asshole. You didn't think to tell me I had a daughter?" Viking's voice was low, and even I could feel the anger vibrating off of him.

Stu's face went white, and I thought the guy might piss himself. "H-h-how did you find out?" He was so freaked out he couldn't even get his words out.

"Karen wrote her a letter before she died. You should have told me years ago."

"Well, now you know. Why the hell are you here?"

The guy must have had a death wish.

"We came to get something she left behind when your sorry ass kicked her out," I announced, while Viper and Colt took off upstairs in search of the photos she had left behind.

"And who the hell do you think you are?" he asked me, with the same false bravado he used with Viking.

"I'm her man, that's all you need to know."

An evil sneer spread across his face when he heard that. "So, she's not that different from her whore mother. Spreading her legs for anyone in a cut."

I didn't know if he was an idiot or knew he wasn't going to get out of this unscathed, but he'd just said the stupidest thing he could, given the situation he was in.

I lunged forward, getting in a few punches to match the ones Viking was already raining down on the fucker.

It didn't take long before he was on the ground, curled up in the fetal position, begging for mercy. After a few more kicks and punches, I felt someone pulling me off of the unmoving lump on the ground.

"Can't let you go down for murder right now," Viper mumbled as he pushed me toward the door.

I watched as Colt did the same with Viking. Once we were both almost out of the house, Colt turned to address the two guys who hadn't made a single move to help their friend. Pussies.

"Do whatever you need here, but if you so much as mention the Desert Sinners, you'll find we won't be as nice next time."

"Right, we didn't see anything," one of them agreed quickly as they moved to check on their friend.

Once we were outside, Viper tossed me the box he must've found in Kate's room. I nodded my head in thanks and placed it in my saddlebag.

"One more stop?" Viking questioned as he got onto his bike.

"One more." I nodded.

We drove a couple of miles to Jonathon's house. Kate had shared enough information about him that it was easy to find where he lived. When we pulled up, I saw his car in the driveway as well. It looked like we were going to be two for two in finding the assholes that hurt my girl.

This time, I led the charge. I knocked on the door, noticing the welcome mat under my feet. Jonathan lived with his mom, and while I needed my message to be clear, I didn't want to freak his mother out. From what Kate had said, his mom always treated her well.

"Hello, can I help you?" A small woman opened the door and looked quite surprised to see us standing on her porch.

"Is Jonathan here?" I tried to keep my voice calm. I didn't need her going into protective mom mode and not be cooperative.

"No, he's not. I'm his mother, Louise Souza," she introduced herself. "Is there something I can help you with?"

"His car's here." I pointed over to the piece of crap sitting in the driveway.

"He just bought a new truck; he hasn't sold his car yet."

I had questioned enough people in my lifetime to know she was telling the truth.

"Any idea where he is?"

"I'm sorry, but what business do you have with Jonathan?"

It was obvious we were starting to scare her.

"I'm Kate's father," Viking jumped in. He was sensing the same thing I was, and I hoped the mention of Kate would encourage her to give us more information.

"Oh." She seemed surprised, but then she squinted her eyes and really looked at Viking. "Wow, you look just like her. It's the eyes." She was smiling. This woman really did like Kate.

Viking smiled and then waited for her to share more about her son's location.

"Well, he's been in Vegas for a week. He left after Kate called him and told him how much she missed him. He said he was driving out to Las Vegas to bring her home. He hasn't been himself since she left."

That was bullshit. There was no way Kate had called him. She'd been ignoring his messages.

"Fuck! We need to get home now before he gets to her!" I yelled as I ran to my bike.

"Jonathan wouldn't hurt her, he loves her," his mom shouted at my back. When I looked at her, I could tell she didn't quite believe her own words.

"Let's go!"

The next two and a half hours were the longest of my life. We had called Wolf and told him that Jonathan was on his way there, and to grab the asshole before he found Kate.

I'd never felt fear like that before.

25

KATE

"Rise and shine."

I could hear a voice, but it sounded distant and a bit muffled. I tried to open my eyes, but the light shining from the bulb hanging from the ceiling was too bright.

"I'm sorry, is that better?" The same voice asked as the light was turned off. When I opened my eyes again, I could see a figure standing by the only window. It was too dark to make out any of the person's features, but I instantly knew who was standing there.

"Jonathan?" I didn't know why I said it like it was a question. There was no doubt in my mind it was him, and I also knew nothing good was going to come from this situation.

"Hello, Kate." His voice didn't sound like that of my old friend. It sounded cold and had an edge to it that scared the crap out of me.

"What happened? Where am I?" My body ached, and when I reached up to touch my head, I quickly pulled my fingers back. There was a large gash that hurt so much, even the tiniest bit of pressure had me seeing stars.

"Seems you had a little bit of an accident."

"Oh my god, Finn and Gunnar! Are they okay?"

"I wouldn't know," Jonathan retorted. "I left those two brats in the car. I don't give a shit about two dumbass kids."

What if they were hurt...or worse?

My head was pounding as memories of the accident came flooding back. Nothing was making sense. I tried to put all the pieces together, but thinking made my head spin and my stomach lurch. "I think I'm going to be sick."

"Not as sick as I was watching you with that criminal." Jonathan started walking toward me, and for the first time since I'd I met him, I was fearful of him.

"You've been watching me?" I asked, trying to get a handle on what was going on. "How long have you been in Vegas? Why are you here?"

Ignoring my question, he continued on his tirade. "I don't understand what possessed you to start acting like such a slut. You were always the good girl. It's why I loved you. Now I don't know what to do with you."

He started pacing the room, and I took the opportunity to check out my surroundings. I needed to find a way out of here. It appeared we were in a house, but it apparently had been abandoned for a while. The mattress I was laying on was bare and smelled musty. There was a table next to me that was covered in a thick layer of dust.

I had no idea how long I had been here. The last thing I remembered was a truck following too close behind me as I drove from Viking and Meredith's house. I was worried about my brothers, and I was praying someone helped them. If someone helped them, then the club would know something happened to me. But even if they knew I was missing, they wouldn't know where to look for me. I needed to find a way out on my own.

After considering my options, I thought it might be best if I tried to talk to Jonathan. If he truly believed he loved me, then maybe I could convince him to not hurt me.

"Jonathan?" He spun around, almost like he forgot I was here while he had been thinking.

"What?"

Everything about him was so different from the guy I knew a couple of months ago. I planned to engage him in conversation, but as he prowled over toward the bed, fear took over.

"I really need to use the bathroom," I blurted out, as an excuse to get away from him.

"Fine, but don't even think about trying to run out of here. I've been nice and not tied you up. Don't make me change my mind."

Running wasn't an option regardless of how much I wanted to. I knew I wouldn't make it very far. That much was clear the moment I stood next to the bed, and the room started to spin. I took a couple of deep breaths and waited a few seconds before attempting to move.

Jonathan led me to the door that was just down the hallway. It was brighter out here with the lights on, and it took a few minutes for my eyes to adjust.

"Don't take too long."

I walked into the bathroom and tried to close the door behind me.

"That's staying open."

There was no way I was going to be able to pee with him watching me. "Please. I promise I'll be quick."

He hesitated for a second. "Fine, but don't do anything stupid. You won't like the consequences."

Never would I have thought Jonathan would be capable of physically hurting me, but this was a side of him I never knew existed. I had no idea what he was capable of.

I needed a few minutes to think. I looked around the bathroom, but there was nothing that would help me in this situation. And there was no way I could squeeze through the tiny window at the top of the wall above the shower.

It was starting to feel like the situation was hopeless.

26

MAC

I followed behind Viking as we headed toward Nevada, but I was shocked when we pulled off the highway just a few minutes outside of town.

"What the fuck are we doing? We need to get home to Kate!" I'd never questioned Viking before, but I wasn't thinking straight. I wouldn't calm down until I knew Kate was safe.

"My phone has been ringing nonstop since we got on the road, but I needed to get us out Apple Valley before Stu went running to the cops," Viking explained.

Viking was right, but I was agitated and just wanted to get back on the road.

"Colt, you call Wolf. Mac, call Kate," Viking continued. "I'm going to call Meredith back."

I looked down at my phone and saw that I didn't have any missed calls. I called Kate's phone, but it went straight to voicemail. I was feeling helpless, something I wasn't used to and never wanted to feel again.

"Meredith, slow down, babe. What happened?"

My attention immediately turned to Viking, and I ran over to him. I could hear Meredith on the other end of the phone. She sounded hysterical, but I couldn't make out what she was saying.

"Shit! Is everyone okay?" Viking's knuckles had turned white, he was gripping the phone so hard. I needed him to hurry up and tell me what was going on.

"Motherfucker," he mumbled under his breath. "We're on our way home now."

As soon as he hung up, I was all over him, trying to get answers.

"There's been an accident. Kate was driving back to her place with the boys when someone hit her car and sent them off the road."

"Fuck! Are they okay? Was it the Phantoms?" I asked, feeling time slipping through my fingers.

"Finn and Gunnar are fine, they're home with Meredith, but the boys said Kate was unconscious. They tried to help her, but someone came along and pulled her from the car."

My mind went to every worst-case scenario imaginable, where Kate was hurt, and I was miles away from home.

Viking placed his hand on my shoulder, grabbing me harder than I expected. "When the boys got out of the car, Kate wasn't there."

"What do you mean she wasn't there? Was she taken to the hospital?" None of what he was saying made sense.

"No," Viking started, and I took a moment to look at him. He was trying to remain calm, but I could tell he was just as freaked out as I was. The dread I'd started to feel was taking over. "No emergency vehicles had shown up yet. The police think whoever pulled her out took her. They questioned the residences and businesses nearest to the accident, and none of them said they saw the Phantoms or gang members."

"It has to be Jonathan. He's obsessed with Kate, and he's MIA." Viking nodded his head in agreement. "We need to get home. Now!" I yelled as I hopped back on my bike.

Typically, we followed behind Viking, but I didn't wait for him to lead. I just prayed the three of them could keep up with me as I hauled ass back to Vegas.

It was late when we got into town. We immediately drove to the accident scene. Kate's car had already been towed away, but a couple of police officers were there, finishing up their investigation.

The minute we were off our bikes, we ran over to them. "Did you guys find anything yet?" Viking barked.

"You need to back the hell up, Viking," Officer Davenport demanded.

We knew Davenport well, and he didn't care much for the club, but he didn't go out of his way to cause trouble for us either.

"My daughter is missing!" Viking yelled. "I want some fucking answers."

"We haven't found anything," Davenport reluctantly explained.

While the two of them argued back and forth, I looked up and down the street, trying to piece anything together. I stopped scanning when I saw the convenience store on the corner.

I started running that way, hoping they had what I was looking for.

"Hi there," the young lady greeted me as I walked up to the counter. "Can I help you?" Her voice shook a bit. I was sure my cut and the intensity showing on my face made her nervous.

"Do you have any surveillance cameras that face the street?"

"Um…we have one that records the parking lot. You can see a little bit of the street on that one."

"Can I take a look at it?"

"I don't know how any of that works," she responded.

"Can you call your boss?"

"O-o-okay."

I watched as she picked up the phone. "Hi, Tom. Sorry to bother you at home. I have someone here who wants to look at some surveillance footage. Can we even do that?" She looked up from the phone to me. "He wants to know who's asking."

"Here, give me the phone," I demanded, holding out my hand.

"Tom? The name's Mac. I need to take a look at that footage. The Desert Sinners would be grateful if you could help us out."

Mentioning the club got his cooperation a lot quicker than explaining the whole situation to him. He gave me a quick rundown of how to get the footage I needed. Just as I was about to go into the back room, Colt and Viper came in.

"Find anything?" Viper asked.

"They have a camera that picks up the street. Gonna check it out."

The three of us sat in the back room messing around with the equipment until we narrowed it down to the time Kate would have left Viking and Meredith's place.

"*Fuck!*" I yelled when I saw her car fly by on the screen. Just a moment later, I could see a white pickup truck follow her. It had to be Jonathan. His mom said he'd just bought a new truck.

I rewound the tape and watched again. We couldn't pick up a license plate number, but at least we had something to go on.

We walked out of the store, saying a quick thank-you to the cashier. When we got outside, I saw Viking jogging toward us.

"I just got off the phone with Wolf. He was able to get ahold of Jonathan's mom, and she was a little more forthcoming with some information. I've got an address to a place Jonathan rented for a couple of days."

"What the fuck are we waiting on? Let's go!"

Viking reached out and pulled me back.

"I need you to get your shit together. I can't have you going in there with guns blazing. My daughter's in there, and I want her safe."

We all nodded in agreement. Even if we knew where she was, we had to play this smart. We had no idea what Jonathan's intentions were, and I wasn't going to risk Kate's safety. One thing was for sure. Tonight, someone was going to die. And it wasn't going to be Kate or any Desert Sinners.

27

KATE

I t was pitch-black outside, and my hopes of finding a way to escape were quickly diminishing. Jonathan had left the room a few minutes ago, and I'd already looked around for anything I could use to help my escape. There was nothing in the room, and I knew I didn't have the strength to fight Jonathan if he caught me. The lights above me kept making this eerie sizzling and buzzing noise that was grating on my nerves.

I prayed that someone had come upon the accident scene and helped Finn and Gunnar. The guilt of not keeping them safe was too much to bear. I couldn't believe I'd brought these problems to Viking's life. What kind of daughter was I?

"What are you thinking about, love?" I heard Jonathan's voice come from the doorway. The use of the word "love" made my skin crawl. His calm, quiet voice scared me even more than his sinister one from earlier.

"I'm not your love," I seethed. There was only one man I would ever belong to, and I wasn't sure I was ever going to see him again.

I probably shouldn't have argued with Jonathan, but I figured he was going to do whatever he wanted with me anyway, and I didn't want to give him the satisfaction of thinking I was his.

"C'mon, don't be like that. We had one little fight. Once we spend some time together again, you'll forget all about this place and realize we're meant to be."

He had to be insane. That was the only explanation for his delusional behavior.

"You're crazy!" I yelled.

I saw the flash of anger in his eyes as he made his way over to the bed where I was still sitting. I moved back as far as my body would allow.

"You're obviously still not thinking clearly," he said as he gripped my jaw tightly, forcing me to look at him. "I've spent too many years waiting for you. I'm done waiting."

"What are you talking about? I told you we could only ever be friends."

"Well, I don't accept that. I'm going to make some dinner, and you can sit in here and think about how being with that criminal hurt me, and how you're going to make it up to me."

Nausea returned with a vengeance, and I was grateful when he walked out of the room. I decided I wasn't going to wait any longer to see what he was going to do. I sat up, taking a moment to let the dizziness fade. I didn't have any weapons, but I was going to do whatever it took to get away from him.

I heard movement in the kitchen and decided to wait by the bedroom door. If I could surprise him, maybe I could hit him hard enough to get a few seconds of lead time and run out of here. It was a risky move, but it was better than lying around here doing nothing.

His footsteps were getting closer, and I could feel my heart pounding in my chest. I crouched down a bit to try to get a little extra leverage and waited to pounce. As soon as I saw his shadow cross over the threshold, I got ready, and when I saw the first hint of his body, I went into attack mode.

I pushed the tray he was carrying into his body, the soup on it spilling all over him. Unfortunately, some of the scalding liquid landed on me as well, but I wasn't going to let the pain slow me down.

"You fucking bitch!" Jonathan yelled as I grabbed the tray. I swung it as hard as I could at his face, then dropped it and ran.

I was almost to the door when I was suddenly pulled backward. The stinging of my scalp where my hair was being ripped out hurt like hell, but I kept fighting. Unfortunately, Jonathan was stronger than I was, and he was able to pull me back down the hallway, even while I was kicking and screaming.

"You really are stupid," he said as he dragged me back up to my feet, then stopped suddenly. "What the hell was that?"

I didn't know what he was talking about. My head was pounding. Then I heard the front door crash open, making me scream.

Before I knew it, Jonathan jerked my body in front of his like a shield and pointed a gun at my head. I had no idea where the gun had come from. When I looked to my left, I saw Mac and Viking standing at the entryway with guns pointed at Jonathan.

My knees went weak, and it took every bit of strength I had to remain upright.

"Put the fucking gun down," Mac instructed. His deep voice scared me, but I could also hear a hint of fear laced in his words.

"This is a bit unexpected." Jonathan chuckled, still not removing the gun from my right temple.

"Let her go!" Viking roared.

"The two of us are meant to be together, and there's nothing either of you can do about it." Jonathan was starting to rant like a lunatic. He was losing control, as was evident by him flailing the gun around to emphasize his words.

"You're going to put the gun down and let her go," Mac repeated. His whole body was tight with anger. "You've got a chance of getting out of this alive, but you need to let her go."

Jonathan started laughing hysterically. "Do you think I'm stupid? You're not going to let me live." Suddenly his voice changed, and I'd never heard anyone look so evil. "But if I can't have her, no one else can either."

Everything from there happened in slow motion, but my eyes stayed on Mac. I heard several shots go off at the same time, and once again, I was thrust into darkness.

28

KATE

The fluorescent lights hanging from the ceiling were making the pain in my head excruciating, but I didn't close my eyes. Instead, I lay there, watching the two most important men in my life sleep on the small sofas the nurses brought in for them after a couple of nights trying to sleep in the hard, plastic chairs.

They hadn't left my side since I was rushed to the hospital with a bullet wound to the shoulder. I was lucky my injury hadn't been more serious. Jonathan hadn't been as fortunate. While a small part of me mourned the loss of a friendship I once held dear, it was clear Jonathan wasn't the same person I once knew. Or perhaps, I'd never known the real him.

"How are you feeling, sweetie?" Meredith asked quietly as she walked into the room, careful not to wake the guys.

"I'm okay."

I may have been in a considerable amount of pain, but I was alive, thanks to Mac and my father. Every time I thought about what they risked to save me, it brought out emotions that were difficult to handle. I owed them everything.

When I woke up after surgery and saw the two of them, I was so relieved neither had been hurt. I asked them if they were going to be arrested for killing Jonathan. I knew I wouldn't be able to live with the guilt if either had to serve time because of me. They assured me it was all taken care of, but they wouldn't give me details. They said it was club business, which drove me crazy.

"The doctor said you might be able to go home tomorrow," Meredith stated, and I nodded my head.

"So, we're busting out of here soon?" Viking asked as he stretched and slowly sat up.

"You don't have to stay," I told him yet again, which earned me a hard glare. Viking had already made it clear he wasn't leaving until I did.

"Hey, baby," Mac said. Our conversation must have woken him up as well. He got off the sofa and walked to my bedside.

"Hi." I smiled at him. Every time I looked at him, my heart skipped a beat. I couldn't believe I'd been lucky enough to not only find a family but also find the man I was meant to be with.

He leaned down to kiss me. He was being gentle, but I wanted more. I reached up and pulled him even closer. I moaned into his mouth, completely forgetting we had an audience until I heard my father clear his throat.

"We're going to get some coffee in the cafeteria," Meredith announced, pulling a reluctant Viking behind her.

"I'll be right back," Viking called from the doorway.

"No, he won't," Meredith stated emphatically. "You two need a little privacy."

I heard my dad grumble all the way down the hallway and it made me laugh.

"That's a beautiful sound, babe."

I looked at Mac. "What's a beautiful sound?"

"That laugh. I was scared out of my mind that I might never hear it again. Seeing a gun pointed at you nearly broke me." I saw his eyes glisten with pure, raw emotion. "I knew then I could never live without you. I love you."

Hearing those words had tears streaming down my face. "I love you more."

And then I kissed my man with all the passion in the world. He may have been a bad biker...an outlaw. But he was mine, and I would forever be his.

EPILOGUE

MAC

Two Months Later

"Do we have to go to the party tonight?" Kate asked as she laid on my chest, gently running her fingernails over my abs.

"Babe, I'm an officer, and we're welcoming one of our charters. I have to at least make an appearance."

"I bet I could tempt you to stay," she said as she started gliding her hand down lower.

"You don't play fair." I grabbed her hand to stop her from starting something I didn't have time to finish. "Let's get up. The sooner we get there, the sooner we can come back here, and I can have my way with you." I smacked her ass as we both got up to get dressed.

Thirty minutes later, we were walking into the clubhouse.

The party was already in full swing, the alcohol flowing and plenty of girls for the visiting club, with one notable absence.

When Viking found out Michelle had told Jonathan where to find Kate when he had come to the clubhouse looking for her, he kicked her out on her ass. She was lucky that getting kicked out was the worst of her punishment.

I couldn't help but feel like Kate's injuries were all my fault. If it hadn't been for me, Michelle wouldn't have had it out for Kate, and Jonathan might not have found her that night. Kate said I was ridiculous and that nothing would have stopped Jonathan. She may have been right, but I was going to do everything within my power to make sure she was always protected.

I grabbed us a couple of beers and led Kate over to the corner. I sat down on the couch and pulled her onto my lap. A few months ago, I would have been participating in the debauchery happening all around us. But now, I was content sitting here with my girl. I would never miss the emptiness that went along with the life I had been living. Not when I knew how it felt to the have the love of a woman as incredible as Kate.

As the night progressed, I talked with a couple of guys from Reno. I met their president, Ice. He came across as an arrogant asshole, but he was here to help us. It was apparent their club was just as fed up with the Phantoms as we were. He had brought a few of his officers with him, as well as his sister. I wasn't sure what the story was with that, but Kate was chatting her up, so I was sure she'd fill me in later.

It was starting to get late, and I wanted nothing more than to get back to the place I now shared with Kate and make good on my promise to fuck her until she couldn't see straight.

"Mac, emergency meeting now," Colt said as he walked by on his way to the back room.

So much for my plan. "Wait here for me, okay?" I asked as I knelt down to kiss Kate.

"Okay," she said against my lips. Fuck, I loved kissing her.

I walked into the room filled with our members and the officers from Reno.

"Everyone, quiet down!" Viking got everyone's attention quickly. "I was just talking to Ice, and we think the Phantoms are planning to make a move sooner than we expected."

A bunch of pissed rumblings rang throughout the room.

"This is some serious shit, boys. I need you all to stay alert and get things at home sorted ASAP. Everyone needs to be ready to ride out at a moment's notice."

I hung back as everyone else started to leave. "If I have to leave, I want Kate to stay with Meredith," I said, not even bothering to ask.

"Of course," Viking responded as he walked to the door. Just as he was about to exit, he turned to look at me. "Shit's about to go down, Mac. I hope you're ready."

The End

ALSO BY RACHEL LYN ADAMS

Life Unexpected Series

Falling for the Unexpected

Loving the Unexpected - Coming Soon

Desert Sinners MC

Mac

Colt - Coming June 2019

ACKNOWLEDGMENTS

Thank you so much for taking a chance on this new series. These MC men have been playing around inside my head for a couple of years, and I'm so happy to finally be telling their stories.

Thank you to my hubby and kids. You guys always encourage me and don't get upset when I lock myself away to write. Love you all more than you know!

To my mama who supports me in so many ways. I have no idea what I would do without you and your words of wisdom.

I still can't believe I'm actually writing books and putting them out there for people to read. I can't thank the readers enough for all the support.

ABOUT THE AUTHOR

Rachel lives in the San Francisco Bay Area with her husband, five children, one dog, four cats, and a bearded dragon. Whenever she has some free time you'll find her with a book in her hands.

Check out my website for information on my upcoming projects.

www.rachellynadams.com

Printed in Great Britain
by Amazon

81807117R00122